W9-AVM-265

THE LIBRARY OF INDIANA CLASSICS

BAD
MAN
BALLAD

Scott R. Sanders

Indiana University Press
Bloomington and Indianapolis

The *Library of Indiana Classics* is available
in a special clothbound library-quality edition
and in a paperback edition.

This book is a publication of

Indiana University Press
601 North Morton Street
Bloomington, Indiana 47404-3797 USA

http://iupress.indiana.edu

Telephone orders   800-842-6796
Fax orders   812-855-7931
Orders by e-mail   iuporder@indiana.edu

Originally published by Bradbury Press
© 1986, 2004 by Scott Russell Sanders
All rights reserved

The paper used in this publication meets the minimum requirements
of American National Standard for Information Sciences—Perma-
nence of Paper for Printed Library Materials,
ANSI Z39.48-1984.

Manufactured in the United States of America

Cataloging information is available from the Library of Congress.

ISBN 0-253-34414-X (cloth : alk. paper) —
ISBN 0-253-21688-5 (pbk. : alk. paper)

1 2 3 4 5 09 08 07 06 05 04

For Barbara and Christer Mossberg

Love was the first motion . . .
—JOHN WOOLMAN

1

FROM THE MOMENT HE OPENED HIS CABIN DOOR and found a coiled blacksnake asleep on the stoop and heard warblers singing, out of season, in the sycamores by the creek, Ely Jackson knew in his bones that today was no day for stirring abroad. Two bad signs at once. Maybe this war had turned the whole of creation sour. On such a day a fellow had better lie low, not go hunting a lost brother. With the toe of his moccasin he nudged the snake until it slid away into the grass. Then he stood watching the woods fill up with light, listening to the warblers. Didn't the fool birds know it was August? The sun was barely up, but already sweat beaded on Ely's forehead and stung the corners of his eyes.

He was about to go inside and fry some turkey for breakfast when a harsh cry cut through the birdsong, like the screech of a file against a sawblade. What on God's round earth was *that*? The birds hushed. He stiffened, held his breath. The screech came again, from up the path toward the village. The only soul within calling distance up that way was the spice girl, who lived by herself in a hut made of woven branches. Thought of the girl and her green eyes made Ely snatch his gun, saddle his horse, and take off riding to see what the trouble was.

Could be a bear or panther scaring her, could be a runaway soldier, or some of those Indians the English sent from Detroit after scalps. His chest seized up with the terror she must feel, a lone girl like that. No family around, no friends that Ely had ever noticed. Could she even shoot a gun? Maybe she cast spells, like people said. She was around his age, seventeen or so, and like him she was an orphan. Some folks called her Marie Antoinette Rozier, after her white father, a Frenchman; others called her Rain Hawk, after her Shawnee mother. Ely had never called her by any name, had never spoken a word with her. But whenever he passed her place he stopped on the trail and hid behind the elderberry bushes to listen if she was singing.

"Get on, Babe," he urged his mare. But she would go no faster than a walk, as if the weight of Ely's fear had settled from his heart into her legs. There were no more shrieks. Again the warblers took up their out-of-season song. When the spice girl's hut came in sight, the mare stopped, ears flattened and nostrils quivering. "What's got *you* spooked?" Ely muttered.

He lifted himself in the stirrups to get a better look, and spotted Rain Hawk at the edge of her clearing. She had her back to him and was bent over her grinding stump, swaying and tugging as if she were pounding corn. Her long hair, black as midnight, was tied in a rag of blue cloth. As she worked, the beads on her skirt glittered. Nothing looked amiss—no bear, no soldiers, nothing to make her scream. He was about to yell halloo, to keep from surprising her, when she swung about and gave him a wild stare. Now how did she know he was there? He waved his hat reassuringly, but she backed away from the stump and went scrambling for the hut, shell earrings flashing. In a moment she ducked inside and lowered a blanket over the doorway.

Ely was not used to scaring people. Tall for his age but lean and gawky, with a head of red hair like a burning bush, ears poking out like question marks, dressed in a wide-brimmed hat and a deerskin shirt, he was usually taken for a wandering portrait painter or a boy evangelist, nobody to run away from. Maybe it was the gun hanging from the saddle. He cupped hands to his mouth and shouted: "I only come to see if you was needing help."

The flap in the doorway hung motionless. Ely hated to think of her crouching inside the hut, peering out at him as if he were a renegade or a wolf. Since the mare would not budge forward, he should have turned right around and headed home. But he had never been able to give up on a puzzle, so he hesitated, casting a suspicious eye at the stump where Rain Hawk had been working. And he saw it wasn't any corn-grinding log sticking out of the hole; it was a pair of legs in boots and black wool breeches. They must belong to some little boy, judging by the length of them, some fool boy who had wandered by and stuck his nose in the stump and managed to get jammed in there head-first. The child must be good and stuck if Rain Hawk couldn't yank him out.

"Easy now," Ely called. "I'm coming." He tethered the balky mare and went on toward the upthrust pair of legs. "You got nothing better to do than climb into stumps, you numskull?"

The legs made no answer. Instead of flailing, they jutted stiffly in the air as if they had sprouted like saplings.

"Playing possum, are you? Tell me, you ever know a possum dumb enough to get wedged in a stump?" Ely grabbed the legs and gave a pull, then pulled harder, for the boy was marvelously stuck. As the weight came free, he almost let it drop again in dismay, for the legs were too thick and the body too heavy and the child unnaturally quiet. Lord lord, he thought, it ain't just playing. It's bad hurt, whatever sort of child it is.

He struggled with the clumsy bulk, let it slip, and the body slumped to the ground with its face in the dirt. "You, child?" Ely bent over the still back. "Child?" Not a sound, nothing but his own hissing breath. He had lifted enough dead bodies to know the feel of one —his father and mother, his sister, his baby brother. He felt no desire to roll the body over, to see the face. Had the child smothered? It wore a suit of black wool, strange getup for anyone in August. And who would put boots on a boy in summer? He was too short to be older than eight or nine years. But it was clear even through his coat that he had the burly shoulders and stout arms of a man.

Kneeling by the body, Ely glanced at one of the outstretched hands, and then he knew for certain that he never should have stirred from the cabin this morning. For the knuckles bristled with gray hair, and the nails were as thick and milky as chips of mica. He glared round at the spice girl's hut, but there was no help to be expected from that quarter. What else could he do but grasp one of those man-muscled arms and tug at the body, knowing even before the face rolled into view with its flat hound-dog nose and ratty beard that this wasn't the body of a child at all, but that of a stunted man, a dwarf.

"God almighty!" Ely swore. He had only seen a dwarf once before, long ago with Pappy at a traveling show in Louisville. This one's face was mashed and bruised. The look on it was vacant, as if death had caught him between emotions. The head was caved in and the arms were twisted loose from their sockets and the chest was a pie of loose muscle and bones. The body looked as though it might have fallen out of the sky. Whatever had shoved the dwarf into that stump had been a good deal stronger than the spice girl. A bear? A gang of men?

He swung around, scanning the woods. Nothing but trees, vines, dappled light. "Who the devil is he?" Ely hollered toward the hut. "How'd he get here? Whatever killed him?"

When no answer came, he approached the hut cautiously. She might just shoot him, or cast a spell on him. There was nothing except his fear of females to keep him from shoving aside the curtain and barging in. For that matter, he hardly needed to use the door.

It was the sort of place you could stand inside and sling a cat outdoors through any wall. Woven of branches, plastered with moss and clay, with bundles of reeds for a roof, the hut was more like a nest than a house. Ely could easily have torn it open and grabbed the girl and shaken an answer from her. But he thought of her melancholy singing, the shells dangling from her ears, the forest color of her eyes, and decided to let her be. Someone else would have to question her—Sheriff Jenkins, maybe, or Mr. Lightfoot, the lawyer.

He gazed back at Babe. He could just climb on her and ride away from this mangled body. Nobody would be the wiser, except the girl watching him from the hut. But for a fellow who was so good at finding trouble, he was not much good at leaving it alone once he had stumbled across it. You start a thing, you finish it, Pappy used to say. So Ely fetched his blanket roll and wrapped the dwarf in it. The body felt like a sack of corncobs on his shoulder, the crushed bones shifting and grating inside the skin. As he came up to the mare with his bundle she skittered nervously, eyes rolling, tugging at the reins. "There now, Babe," he murmured, "there, there," rubbing her behind the ears. Before she could dance away he flung the dwarf across the saddle. "Easy. Easy now. Don't like the smell of this, eh? Want nothing to do with it? I don't blame you one bit. You've got more sense than I do." Presently she settled down, and with the saddle rope Ely tied the body to the pommel.

Not bothering to yell any more questions at the

spice girl, he led the mare toward Roma. But as he passed the hut, Rain Hawk shrieked through the flimsy walls, "Leave the rabbit here! I will bury him! And don't follow the bearman!"

"What do you mean, *bearman?*" Ely shouted. He waited. "Now listen, you come on out here and explain this business to me! I'm nothing to be afraid of! Just come on out here!"

The girl would not emerge from her nest. Well, then, he would drive her out. He searched the ground for a rock to heave at her doorway. Spying one next to a mud hole, he bent down to seize it, but caught himself in mid-motion, his heart jumping. There in the damp earth was a huge bootprint, maybe eighteen inches long. He jerked upright, spun around staring into the woods. Nothing, nothing. Then he looked back at the print. He found that his own two moccasins fit inside it end-to-end.

The back of his neck prickled. "Great God almighty!" he swore again, this time in a whisper. These weren't a man's bootprints, they were a giant's. Whoever or whatever had made them was heavy in proportion, because even in the dry stretches of the trail, now that he bothered to look, the prints showed clearly, two yards apart. Ely followed them backward, and they led first to the grinding stump, then to the hut. In the mud near the doorway, scattered among the huge tracks were the prints of tiny boots. Dwarf boots. Kneeling to study them, imagining Rain Hawk crouched on the other side of the curtain, Ely could see that the dwarf had approached the hut first, followed by the giant. But only the giant had walked away.

Bearman? What on earth did she mean by that? He turned around and followed the monstrous prints forward, leading the mare by the reins, all the time trying to imagine what he would do if and when he caught up with the owner of those boots.

Beyond the next turn in the path, where on other mornings he would breathe deeply to smell the cedars, Ely caught his breath. Another body lay sprawled in the dirt, a body shorter than the dwarf and just as stout, inspiring in him a vision of midget corpses trailing ahead, each body more compact than the previous one, and the murderer's tracks swelling with each victim, until the last body of all would be as dense and round as a cannonball.

But no, he realized, drawing closer, it was only a rucksack. Made of hide, a yard long and crammed full, laced to a frame of bent hickory, the pack must have weighed a hundred pounds. The bearman had carried it this far, that was clear from the tracks, and then had set it down in the middle of the road. Opening the flap, Ely found scissors, needles, thread, combs, salt, spices, harness buckles, flints—all the truck of a peddler.

And who was the peddler? Surely the dwarf could never have lifted the rucksack, let alone carried it. But if it belonged to the giant, why did he drop it here, and why on earth did he kill the dwarf? No telling. All laws of science and common sense broke down when you came to dealing with freaks of nature.

Grunting from the weight, Ely shoved the rucksack

onto the mare's rump behind the dwarf. Babe gazed around at him with eyes like slick chestnuts. The huge prints continued on up the trail, and so did Ely, tugging at the reins and thinking, why didn't this happen to somebody grown, somebody with a pappy alive to call for help, somebody without a runaway brother to find?

The trail soon dipped downhill, then vanished into Bone Creek. The bootprints vanished, too. Ely waded his mare across the shallow creekbed, hooves clattering on the shale, but on the other side he could find no tracks. The big guy could have waded all the way to Lake Erie without lifting his boots from the water. Hope to heaven he did, thought Ely. Let him go haunt some other territory. Yet now, peering down at the gray shale of the creekbed, where even giants left no tracks, he never thought of giving up the chase. Instead he tethered his mare and waded half a mile up Bone Creek, then half a mile down, studying both banks as he went. Finding no more bootprints, he decided to leave off the hunt until he had told folks in the village and had shed himself of the rucksack and the dwarf.

As he drew within sight of the horse he saw Rain Hawk working at the knots in the rope, trying to untie the wrapped body. He ran hard, shouting, "Hey, you let that alone!"

She dashed into the woods. From somewhere back in the brush, she called, "Leave the rabbit for me and I will bury him! Do not follow the bearman!"

He tore after her through the trees, stumbling over

roots, smacking into low branches, guided by the sound of her running footsteps and her clacking beads, meaning to seize her and drag her to the village if need be, girl or no girl. But she was as quick as a fox, and soon gave him the slip. He wound up back at the creek beside the mare, an ache in his side and a black fury in his heart.

In a few minutes his breath had smoothed out, but not his temper. Lord, she was aggravating. And so was the dwarf. Why did he have to get himself murdered right next door? But those oversized bootprints went beyond aggravation. They were a pure wonder, too baffling to put out of mind. All the way into Roma, where he would deliver his horseful of worrying, strange items, Ely thought about those marvelous prints, remembering how one of them had swallowed his own two feet.

2

A SKYFUL OF CLOUD PRESSED DOWN OVER ROMA like a lid on a kettle, sweltering and heavy. The breath in Ely's throat felt like warm syrup. Before reaching the village square he and the laden mare were encircled by a crowd. First came the children, eager for any distraction, then mothers, gasping in the muggy air, babies clinging to their hips, sweat darkening their dresses in half-moons under the arms, and finally the few men who were not in the fields or away at the war, men rangy as backwoods hogs, their hands dangling from the sleeves of hunting shirts. Ely and the mare scuffled to a halt within the circle of curious eyes.

"What you got there?" people asked, fingering the rucksack and the wrapped bundle.

"Items for Sheriff Jenkins and nobody else," Ely said.

"Sheriff's likely home napping this time of day," said Asher Gurley, the blacksmith, a man with a face as pitted as cinders.

"Then let me through to the lawyer's office," Ely said.

But the circle held, and questions flew at him from all sides. "Is it stolen goods? English gunpowder? Pelts? A dead Indian?" Hands fumbled at the pack, each person imagining it full of what was most needed—plow tips, flea powder, Baltimore eyeglasses, Boston newspapers, butcher's reviver, snuff—anything that was hard to come by on this side of the mountains.

"It's peddler's gear," said Ely. "Now kindly get out of my road and let me deliver this stuff to Mr. Lightfoot. Then you can ask him questions until the geese fly north, for all I care."

A little girl who had been peeking into the bundle suddenly shrilled, "It's somebody in there! I can see hair sticking out!"

The questions boiled quickly into shouts. Over the racket Ely bellowed, "Look, it's somebody dead, but I don't know who he is or how he got that way."

Dead! Dead! He's got a corpse in there!

Ely shoved ahead through the sizzle of voices, hurrying across the square toward the lawyer's shingle with Babe trotting behind and the villagers swarming about him.

The office of Owen Lightfoot, Esquire, was the only brick building in Roma, and except for the courthouse it covered the most ground. Its window and door were inset with plate glass that had been hauled up the Mahoning River from Pittsburgh. "One day this will be a city," he was fond of predicting, waving his white-cuffed hands at the huddle of log cabins. He had been entertaining the same hope since coming out to Ohio from Philadelphia in 1809. But in 1813 you could still just about spit across town and you could shoot wolves

on the square at midnight. He was still the only lawyer in the place, and even so he was mostly idle. In
the four years of his practice, spending more than he
earned, he had nearly run through the small legacy
that had enabled him to set up the brick office to begin with. Yet Roma showed no signs of becoming a
city. In fact, if the militia didn't beat the British on
Lake Erie, and if Tecumseh's league of Indians didn't
fall apart, and if ague and smallpox didn't relent, and
if strangers didn't quit turning up dead on every road
into town, Roma would soon be abandoned to the
grapevines and the vultures.

Owen Lightfoot thought of himself as a man wor-
thy of a grander setting—London, for instance. Much
as he regretted England's role during the Revolution
and her present alliance with the savages up north, he
was nonetheless an admirer of all things British. One
had to respect a civilization that could produce Sir
Isaac Newton and jurisprudence and William Wordsworth and tea. Owen was certainly built on a scale
appropriate to a larger place. His waistcoats and
starched shirts could not conceal his bulk, which the
villagers estimated at roughly two hundred pounds.
A glance through his office window into the street
was sufficient reminder that this was a country of
scrawny men and women, who were driven so hard
clearing land and protecting hogs that they had no
chance of padding their bodies with spare flesh. Owen
could read in their eyes a mistrust of his bulk, as if
fat were a sign of bad faith, a failure of belief in next
year's crop, proof that he was not one of them.

Pursued by the crowd, Ely showed up presently at

this gentleman's door. Motioning for others to carry the rucksack, he lifted the body and pushed his way into the lawyer's office. Some dozen grown-ups, plus dogs and children, squeezed through the door behind him.

Owen had been cleaning his spectacles when the door burst open. He looked at the mob with alarm, recognizing faces he had battled in court. What did they want? Nervously he fitted the glasses to his nose and swept his desk clear of papers.

Ely lurched forward and plumped his burden onto the gleaming walnut desk. The bundle had taken on the shape of a horseshoe from having sagged over the saddle. He took off his hat and mashed it against his chest, announcing, "Here you go, sir."

The lawyer grimaced. "Here goes what, precisely?"

"A body," Ely said. "I found it jammed in a hominy stump close to where Bone Creek crosses the Cairo Trace." He was about to mention the exact spot—out front of Rain Hawk's place—but a recollection of the girl's wild stare and frightened cries made him hold his tongue. Waving forward the two men who were lugging the rucksack, he added, "And this here was laying nearby."

Owen sniffed. The pack smelled of spices, but the filthy bundle smelled only of horse. The body could not have been dead long, not in this brutal heat. "Let's have a look at it, then."

Ely peeled away the blanket to reveal a stubby arm and burly shoulder.

"It sure is an odd-looking child," someone observed.

"That's just what I thought." Ely gave another tug, and the face rolled into view, with its crushed skull and shattered mouth and sparse beard.

There were moans and gasps. Somebody growled, "What in tarnation *is* it?"

"A dwarf, that's what," said Jabez Gilbert, a wagon-driver with wooden teeth who had gained wisdom from traveling.

While the others surged forward to get a better look, Owen tilted back in his chair. He shoved the spectacles onto his forehead and rubbed each eye with a forefinger. In the momentary darkness he thought, as he often did in ugly times, of his youth in Phila-delphia. Would civilization ever make its way over the mountains from that Quaker city to this squalid settlement? Opening his eyes, he said, "What a wretched thing to turn up."

"Should I have left him for the wolves?" Ely de-manded.

"No, no, of course not." Standing up, Owen boomed in his courtroom voice, "Will someone go wake the sheriff?"

At that moment Sheriff Jenkins, a cautious elderly man with an indoor face the color of turnips, shrewd at getting himself elected and at keeping out of harm's way, was being ushered into the office by his vigilant wife. "What is it now?" he asked.

Ely told about finding the dwarf and rucksack, but once again a deep reluctance kept him from mention-ing the spice girl. As for the bootprints, he only said they were unusual but did not mention their size, afraid the listeners would scoff at him. He spoke in a self-conscious mutter, and kept rubbing his red hair as if trying to set it on fire. He stared at the floor from eye sockets that were set so deep in his face they resembled knotholes pounded through a board.

Listening, Owen tried to place this boy with the flaming hair. Wasn't he the one who'd wandered into town last spring, asking about some lost brother? Showing a crude picture, saying, *That's him, my brother Ezra, looks about like me only bigger and older and better-looking?* Yes, Owen remembered now, the boy had picked up some rumors of the brother here in Roma, had stayed around all summer, feeding himself by hunting, sleeping out in the abandoned Needham place. Despite the shadowy sockets, Owen could see in the boy's eyes a look of homelessness and hurt.

"So I figured I'd better carry him on into town," Ely concluded, "to find out what to do."

The sheriff squinted at the body from a distance. "He ain't necessarily been murdered. I've seen worse from accidents."

"It wasn't no accident stuffed him in that stump," Ely said.

"Does anybody know who he is?" Owen asked.

"I don't know him by name," a voice called, "but I'm thinking I seen him before." Pushing through the crowd came Habakuk Bennett, a keelboat man with a mule's long-jawed and gloomy face. He bent over the dwarf a moment. "Yessir, I seen him awhile back in Pittsburgh, outside a foundry, and he had this here pack with him. He was standing there when the men come off work from the furnaces, his fist in the air

[16]

full of money, like this, calling, 'Anybody want to earn cash money for carrying my goods through the woods of Ohio?' " Bennett pondered the squashed face. "Yessir, you won't see two of them in a lifetime."

"And did he hire himself a foundryman?" Owen inquired.

"That I can't tell you," said Bennett. "I never saw."

Talk of foundrymen reminded Ely of those outrageous prints. Once, passing through Wheeling on the trail of his brother, he had watched men working naked before the open furnaces, shoveling tons of ore, pouring cauldrons of liquid iron into molds, hefting cast plows and anvils and stoves. But even in the foundry Ely had never seen a man big enough to leave such tracks.

"Let's see if he carried any identification." Owen groped inside the dwarf's coat and drew out a wad of bank notes, setting off a chorus of whistles in the cramped office. "He doesn't appear to have been robbed, whether or not he was murdered."

"That money's under my custody," the sheriff announced.

"You better count it first!" shouted a skeptic in the crowd, and others murmured amen. Owen obligingly counted the bills aloud. While the numbers tolled out, Ely glanced at the door to see if the clouds had broken. When he caught a glimpse of blue, he thought for a moment it was clear sky, and then he recognized the blue rag, the midnight hair, the earrings of polished shell. From the door, where she was standing on a chair to peer over heads, Rain Hawk returned his stare. She mouthed something at him, a look pleading and angry at the same time. What possesses the girl? He motioned her toward the desk, but she leaped down from her chair, spun around, and darted away into the street.

Owen proclaimed a total of seven hundred and twelve dollars.

The buzz of astonishment grew louder. Why, you could buy a thousand acres with that much money. What fool would have killed someone and then left a fortune on the body?

From other pockets in the suit Owen extracted a glass vial of perfume, a pistol, a bill of sale from a Pittsburgh butcher, and a card testifying that the undersigned had been saved on June 12, 1811, in Portsmouth, New Hampshire. The signature, boldly stroked, identified one Epaphrus Matthews.

"Let's see what Mr. Matthews had to peddle." Owen dumped the contents of the rucksack onto his desk and began sorting hinges and spools and looking glasses into neat piles, the way he sorted words or ideas.

"Those goods are under my custody," Sheriff Jenkins declared, but nobody paid him any mind.

When all the trinkets were in view, people wondered aloud how any man who dealt in such trifling wares could have saved up seven hundred dollars.

"You mentioned finding some unusual bootprints near the body," Owen said, picking up on the one detail that Ely had refused to elaborate. "What was remarkable about them?"

"They were awful big," Ely admitted grudgingly.

"How big?"

"Big enough to hold my two feet stuck end-to-end."

This revelation set off a general exodus down the Cairo Trace in the direction of Bone Creek. Even the lawyer, who rarely stirred from town, rode out to examine these wonderful tracks. But there were no bootprints of any description to be found, for the trail between the creek and the stump had been swept with a twig broom. The mud hole in which Ely had first discovered the gigantic print was now smooth, showing only the faint claw marks of the twigs. Ely searched the ground in circles, like a bird-dog sniffing for a trail, hoping the spice girl had missed one bootprint. But she had done her work thoroughly. In the clearing where the hut should be was only a heap of brush. "Well, I'll be dadburned," he muttered.

The others clustered around him, some on horseback, most afoot. Children climbed onto the stump to peer inside for blood.

Sitting uncomfortably astride his horse, Owen declared, "It appears that someone has been destroying your evidence."

"It sure does look that way," said Ely.

"Wasn't this the site of Mademoiselle Rozier's house?" Owen asked, remembering having ridden out here to buy salves and herbal teas from the spice girl.

"Used to be," Ely said.

"She was here a day ago," said Mrs. Forbes, the Englishwoman who kept house for Owen. "I purchased some pennyroyal from her."

"I seen her in town this noon!" shouted one of the children. "The medicine gal in all her bangles!"

"Perhaps we should locate her and ask whether she's

the one who has so carefully tidied up the road," Owen suggested.

Ely recalled that morning's chase through the woods. "Good luck catching her."

The sheriff spat in the dust. "Looks like that's that."

"Oh no, oh no, she didn't sweep the whole blessed woods," Ely said, whereupon he set off at a trot for the creek, waded in, and went splashing upstream, studying the sand and mud. The crowd trailed after him along the banks or in the water, the children foremost, glad for wet feet, the women lifting their skirts, the men carrying their moccasins or boots. Owen chose to pick his way along the shore, where cockleburrs stuck to his coatsleeves and briars snagged in his shirt.

Ely was beginning to wonder if he had guessed the wrong direction, or if the bearman really had waded all the way to Lake Erie, when he spied the huge prints of naked feet leading up a clay bank from the creek. A triumphant shout burst from him. He had not imagined those amazing tracks after all.

The villagers hunkered down beside the prints, whistling and muttering, and measured them by the spans of fingers. Two little girls planted their four bare feet inside one of the tracks and clung to one another, squealing with astonishment.

"What we got ourselves here is a giant," observed Asher Gurley, who still wore his blacksmith's apron. "Wish I had two good legs to go after him." He slapped his gimpy leg, which had kept him from joining the militia up at Cleveland.

"Somebody must catch him," said Mrs. Forbes. "I

couldn't sleep at night while something that big is loose in the woods."

Heads swiveled toward Sheriff Jenkins, who had kept aloof. "If I go chasing every suspicious character who passes through the county," he protested, "who's going to protect the town?"

Ely took a deep breath. He had no business taking off after some hulking stranger. What would he do if he caught him? And what about finding Ezra? But Ezra's trail was cold. Not a hint of him in these parts for weeks. As likely stumble across him while looking for the giant. Besides, Ely could not get those marvelous prints out of his mind. He just had to see what sort of creature belonged to those feet. "I reckon I'll go," he said.

They all looked at him. Then Asher Gurley said, in a kindly way, "Ain't you a bit young?"

"Reckon I'll find out if I am or not," said Ely.

"Then you got to have somebody go along with you." The blacksmith gazed at the crowd. "Who'll go?" Men shifted from foot to foot. The reasons they gave for sticking at home touched upon the corn harvest, the militia's call to join Harrison in his march on Detroit, the Indian troubles, sick children, sore backs. Ely couldn't blame them. Who in his right mind would chase a murdering giant into the wilderness in the middle of a war?

At last Owen cleared his throat in the formal way he had. "I would be happy to accompany you, Ely."

Everyone gaped at him as if he had just offered to fly. There he stood in his boiled shirt and gold eyeglasses, his body shaped like a summer squash, his hands soft. Behind the lenses his eyes looked like something pickled. So far as anybody knew, he had never so much as slept overnight in the woods.

"You?" Ely demanded.

"And why not? Someone has to represent the law."

"Begging your pardon, sir, but it seems a crazy thing."

"Then we'll be partners in craziness, won't we?" Owen's face set firm above his starched collar, above the black bows of his velvet tie.

3

THE TRUTH WAS THAT OWEN LIGHTFOOT HAD LONG
dreamed of going exploring. Among his earliest
memories was the view from his parents' home on
Society Hill in Philadelphia down to the waterfront,
where oceangoing ships pointed their masts at the stars.
No sooner had he learned to walk than he was stealing down to hide among the bales and crates on the
wharf, listening to sailors cry out in a dozen languages. The air, stirred by wheeling gulls, smelled of
cotton, rum, damp rope, and sun-heated boards. The
eyes of the sailors were filled with distances.

Young Owen taught himself to read even before
enrolling in the Quaker school, he was so impatient
to study the journals of Columbus and Marco Polo,
Hakluyt's *Voyages*, the biographies of Magellan and
Hudson and Cook. Worried lest the boy grow up to
be a swearing sea captain or pirate, his father, who
was a banker, apprenticed him to a judge. There was
nothing like study of the law to wring the adventure
out of a boy. Soon Owen began having nightmares

in which legal sentences coiled like snakes about his neck and gavels pounded on his skull.

What turned him away from dreams of ocean voyaging, however, was not the law's suffocating tangle, but his own queasy stomach. Even sitting in a dinghy on a duck pond made him nauseous. He could not bear to spend five minutes aboard a ship at anchor in the harbor. He prayed to God for strength, performed abdominal exercises, drank tonics guaranteed to put iron into the lining of his stomach. But all to no avail. So he abandoned hope of a career on the ocean and turned his vagrant yearnings inland.

While he was supposed to be copying the judge's papers or studying the Pennsylvania statutes, he browsed instead through Bartram's *Travels* and Catesby's *Natural History*, read the Jesuit *Relations*, pored over maps of the American interior. He spent free afternoons in Mr. Bartram's botanical garden, leaning against some exotic tree and reading poetry about nature. The *Lyrical Ballads* of Mr. Wordsworth sent chills through him. "She shall be sportive as the fawn," he chanted, "that wild with glee across the lawn or up the mountain springs." He imagined himself hiking with the poet beside lakes and roaring cataracts. Or he would visit Mr. Peale's museum to look at the stuffed animals—an orangutan from Borneo, monkeys from Africa, a long-nosed anteater from South America, a great shaggy ox from the North Pole. But the specimens that captivated him were those from his own land, the weasel and fox, the bald eagle mounted with outspread wings, the badger and beaver and timber wolf, animals whose wild cousins actually roamed the endless woods to the west.

Owen thus became an avid mental traveler, but only an indifferent lawyer. While clients droned on about contested wills and civil suits, his imagination journeyed westward through canebrakes and prairies. All that kept him in Philadelphia, aside from obedience to his father, was his fear of the wilds, for however bold Owen was in mind, he was exceedingly timid in body. He knew that neither medicine nor exercise would remedy this weakness. A person was either born with courage, or he was not. In his own case, he had always accepted the verdict of his father, overheard one day when Owen had fainted at the sight of a frog: "The boy is an utter and unmitigated calf."

Resigned to an armchair life, Owen was on the verge of buying his own house atop Society Hill and proposing marriage to an English lady, when two events conspired to alter his future. The first was his father's death under the wheels of a carriage driven by a slave-trader who resented the old man's abolitionist opinions. The second was the arrival in Philadelphia of the animals and plants collected in the far west by Meriwether Lewis and William Clark. Owen had been reading newspaper accounts of their journey, trying to follow their route across America on his maps, which showed the land west of the Mississippi as a blank. When Lewis and Clark's animals were put on display behind the State House, Owen stood entranced, watching them, forgot to appear in court, neglected his sweetheart. There were prairie dogs, coyotes, a rabbit with ears as long and pink as a child's forearm, a squawking bird called the magpie, amazing creatures that had existed, unknown to science, from the beginning of time.

Any chance that he might stay put in Philadelphia was erased by the delivery of the last crates from Lewis and Clark. These contained a stuffed buffalo with curving horns and the awesome cadaver of a grizzly bear. Owen rushed from the courtroom to have a look, and once he had stared at the buffalo and grizzly, he immediately began making plans to head west. With or without courage, he would have to go, or he would die from his knowledge of the world's strangeness and immensity.

From travel books he knew he would need collecting boxes, a telescope, a compass, a portable desk, an umbrella, and guns. By the time he had gathered this equipment, there was no need of explaining matters to his sweetheart, who had already attached herself to a merchant; his few clients had sought out more sensible lawyers. Free to go, in May 1809 Owen climbed into the carriage and ordered his driver to point the horses west.

After the carriage rattled to pieces on the stony roads, he bought a wagon. When the mountains shattered the wagon, he threw out half his goods, including most of his law books, and loaded the rest onto mules. While Owen followed on horseback, a teamster drove the mules to Pittsburgh. Only the pall of smoke hanging over that city kept him from stopping there, exhausted. To continue west from there one had to ride rivers, and so, despite his uneasy stomach, he hired a flatboat. His passion to see the wilderness led him on into Ohio, pushing up smaller and smaller rivers, determined to keep going until he had found the last settlement this side of the savages.

In this fashion, without having fired his rifle or seen any beast larger than a fox or conversed with a sober Indian, he glided up Bone Creek one summer day into the shabby cluster of cabins that some ambitious soul, smitten by the study of Latin, had named Roma. Owen debated whether to face about and hunt elsewhere for a place somewhat further removed from the state of nature. But his boatmen deserted him there, so there he stayed. "One day Roma will be a city," he proclaimed, helping his prophecy along by ordering the construction of a two-story edifice of brick to house himself and his law practice.

He kept meaning to explore the nearby woods, where panthers and Indians still roamed, but first he had to persuade the villagers—who cared little for law, preferring to settle their quarrels in the old muscular way with flintlock and fist—that a lawyer was a useful addition to their community. Between these distractions and his fitful practice and his timidity, he allowed four years to pass without sticking his nose into the woods.

Therefore, when Ely Jackson presented him with that grotesque corpse, revealed the monstrous bootprints, and volunteered to follow wherever they led, Owen was so ripe with yearning that he offered to go along. In Ely he saw a younger version of himself, but one who had never grown fat, never learned fear, a born explorer. If such a boy can dare the wilderness, thought Owen, so can I. Despite the impeccable logic of this decision, which had been predestined from the day he watched sailors dancing on the yardarms of ships, no one was more astonished by his foolhardy offer than Owen himself.

Drawn by news of the murder, people trickled into Roma from the countryside. By late afternoon more faces were gathered in the muddy square outside the lawyer's office than at any time since the announcement, a year earlier, of the latest war with England. Outlandish tales buzzed through the crowd. Stupefied by the heat, children stopped squirming and listened while grown-ups told stories about the Old People, the Mound Builders, who had lived in Ohio long before the Shawnee or Miami. When one of the burial mounds had been dug up for clay to make brick, the diggers had found a human skeleton seven feet long. Bearmen, the Indians called these vanished giants, because once in a great while the spirit of a Mound Builder would grow angry and take on the shape of a bear and go stalking about at night, wrecking entire villages. "That is called a bearwalk," said an old Shawnee man, "and only spirit weapons can save you from it."

"Giants!" squealed a toddler, overhearing the word, his eyes swollen wide as watches. *Giants, giants,* other voices took it up. Standing in the shade of the lawyer's office, men speculated on the best methods for killing such a creature. Women debated whether to

pack up their households and head back east. Children kept whispering, *"A dwarf and a giant!"*

Owen tried to set his paperwork in order while the crowds shuffled by his desk examining the corpse. Only after he had persuaded several men to carry the body and rucksack to the sheriff's office was he left in peace. On each document he penned a note, instructing Mrs. Forbes what to do with it should he not return from his expedition. Leaving his dear housekeeper was for Owen the most troubling aspect of this madcap venture. The elegance of her speech and dress and manners kept him from losing touch with civilization out here in the hinterlands, where people wore the skins of animals and spoke in grunts. Because she was so ill-suited to this raw territory, he feared she might run away. More than once he had thought of marrying her, but marriage seemed to him nearly as mysterious and fearful as the wilderness. "Dear Mrs. Forbes," he wrote on the last document, "please wait for me." Sweat from his nose blurred the ink.

Meanwhile, Ely had to see to his own preparations. From four years of roving about in search of his brother, he knew only too well the routines of departure. First rub down Babe, check her shoes, load her oats and cracked corn into saddlebags. While he worked he apologized in advance for the miseries he would be putting her through. "Who knows where we'll catch up with the bigfoot," he told her. "Maybe China, with him covering six feet of ground at every step." To soothe her, he played a few tunes on his flute. Next, there was the knapsack to load with food, the hunting pouch to load with possibles—flint and steel, grape-vine bark for tinder, tallow candles and resiny pine knots for light, skillet and fork, tin cup, linen packing for the gun.

The gun, of course, was always ready, but he needed to buy a supply of balls and powder. Since he had to traipse into Roma for that, and since everything he owned was now on Babe's back, he decided he might as well stay overnight in town. On the way there he paused at Rain Hawk's clearing, but the only sign of her was that heap of brush, like the scattered twigs of a squirrel's nest. Where in blazes had she gone? Chasing a man, no matter how big his feet, was a piece of work Ely could understand. But chasing a girl was beyond him. That chore he would leave to the lawyer, who seemed unlikely to be of any other use.

He found the lawyer's office cluttered with items the villagers had brought—and were still bringing—for the trip. Pies, jugs, ropes, blankets, lumpy sacks. While Ely gaped at all this gear, the blacksmith delivered a heavy set of manacles.

"We're going on horses, not boats," Ely pointed out.

"Never know what you'll need," said Asher Gurley.

Others kept trudging in with supplies, as if they were preparing the lawyer's office for a siege.

At this rate, thought Ely, we'll be needing a stagecoach. "Where's Mr. Lightfoot?" he asked. A woman carrying a slab of bacon pointed at the ceiling. So he went outside, where the evening air felt like the breath of furnaces, and climbed the outside stairway to the lawyer's apartment on the second floor and rapped at the door. Receiving no answer, he knocked harder.

Presently Mrs. Forbes opened it, her eyes wet. "Yes?"

Aware in the woman's presence of his work-blackened hands, his patched deerhide clothes, his swampy smell, Ely raised his broad hat and stammered, "Evening, ma'am," and was still holding the hat aloft when Owen came out to meet him, a clutch of daisies in one fist and a look of turmoil on his face.

"I thought we agreed to leave in the morning," said Owen.

"I just wanted to see how you're coming with the packing."

Mrs. Forbes stepped onto the landing beside Ely. "If you've made up your mind, Mr. Lightfoot, I won't stoop to pleading."

"My dear," said Owen. The daisies drooped from his fist.

She started down the stairs, her long skirts brushing the treads. "I hope you survive your little jaunt."

"You *will* wait?" Owen called after her.

She gave no answer.

Remembering his hat, Ely lowered it, but still gazed after the departing back of Mrs. Forbes. He had never been that close to such a woman in his life. She might have come from Egypt, she was so strange to him, with her flounces and painted lips and the way she talked like a bird singing. If I ever get me a house to look after, he thought, that's the sort of woman I'd want to do the looking.

"I didn't mean to barge in on anything," he said.

Owen flung the handful of daisies over the railing. "It can't be helped now, then, can it?" he said sharply. "Come on in, since you're here."

The floor was piled with satchels. "What's all this truck here?" Ely said, peering into the case where Owen had packed his copies of Gibbon's *Decline and Fall* and Wordsworth's poetry, as well as the telescope, compass, and other scientific items.

"Those are my books and instruments."

"Books? Instruments?" Hefting a wooden box inlaid with mother-of-pearl, Ely added, "And how about this?"

"My traveling desk."

"And this?"

"An umbrella."

"What's it for?"

Owen sighed. "It's for keeping off the rain. And now, if you don't mind, Ely, I can manage my own luggage very well."

Just then footsteps sounded on the stairs. Both had the same thought: Is it Mrs. Forbes come back to patch things up? But no, the woman standing there when the door opened was a stranger to Ely, and Owen had only seen her once before, having watched her buy some Neet's Elixir one day from a wagon in the street. He remembered how she had retrieved her pennies from a knotted handkerchief. Now she stood in the doorway, rocking side to side, as if teetering on the edge of some decision.

"May I help you?" Owen ventured.

"The runt that's dead in the courthouse," she said, "well, I saw him alive yesterday about sunup."

"You did? Where?" said Owen.

"At our place, out Cairo Trace near Seely's Wash." She twisted both hands in her skirts. "There come a knocking at the door before it was light out, but I was wide awake, nursing the baby. My oldest boy opened up, and there was this runt standing there, he didn't even come high as my chest, wearing a store suit and a smile on him like a razor." The woman slewed her skirts around, brooming dust from the lawyer's carpet.

"And what did he want?" Owen coaxed her.

"It was just me and the children. My husband's away at the war." She caught her lower lip between her teeth. "Oh, he ain't going to like these doings at all."

"What doings?" said Ely, growing impatient.

She disentangled her hands from the skirt and began plucking at a sleeve. "Well, the runt says he's got perfume and jewelry and notions for sale, and would I like to buy some. The only money I had in the house was what we'd saved to pay off the land, and I wasn't going to spend it on gewgaws. No, sir, and thank you, I tell him. Then he says would I like to see a freak that he's got waiting outside. Not one bit, I say, but the kids are jumping and yelling yes, and before I can shut them up the runt gives a whistle and stands back out of the door. Then I see this thing out by the corncrib . . ." Her voice died in mid-sentence.

"What was it? What?" said Ely.

"I couldn't see too good on account of the sun wasn't all the way up, but it looked like a man—least it stood on its hind legs—only it was way too big for a man, tall as the corncrib. The head was huge and furry, and it looked all humpbacked."

"Humpbacked?" said Owen. "Do you suppose this —this creature—might have been carrying a large pack?"

"Could be," the woman said. "All I know is I didn't want it coming any closer to me and my children. And the runt says for a dollar he'll have his freak come in here and do a show for us. 'It's my ironman,' he says, 'my Pennsylvania ironman. He can lift a wagon over his head without so much as a grunt. Breaks bodies in two over his knee. He'll do any sweet little thing I tell him.' No no no, I say, and this time the kids are screaming no. But he gives a whistle anyway, and this ironman of his starts heading for the cabin. 'Or give me a few dollars more and I'll call him off,' says the runt. Then I start pulling money from the crock, keep on pulling until the crock is empty. And by then the cabin's dark, the doorway is filled with this ironman. All you can see is from the chest down, a hunting shirt and leggins just like a man's. And the baby's in my arms wailing and the children are holding on to me and there's not a penny more to give. Then the runt stuffs the money in his coat, backs out of the cabin grinning, and I jump up and bar the door."

"You didn't get any better look at the big one?" said Ely.

The woman shook her head doggedly. "I didn't want a better look. All I wanted was to bar that door." Her eyes saucered with tears. "My husband's going to lay into me for giving over that money."

[34]

Ely, who did not have five dollars to his name, was on the point of offering to find her the money somehow, when Owen declared, "Don't you worry. I feel certain you'll be paid back from the funds we discovered on this man's body. I wouldn't be surprised if he robbed others as he robbed you."

Like maybe Rain Hawk? Ely wondered, remembering the two sets of bootprints, the one huge and the other tiny, leading up to the spice girl's hut. The dwarf's tricks had run out on him there. But why? Did the ironman turn on him and mash him like a frog into that stump? And if so, was it Rain Hawk who turned the big man on his master?

After the woman had left, Ely made a bed for himself on the lawyer's floor, and carried these questions with him into sleep.

Before retiring, Owen wrote an additional note to Mrs. Forbes, asking her to look after the woman whom the dwarf had robbed, and to keep a list of any others who might come forward with similar tales, and to wait, please wait. As he was sprinkling sand on the wet ink, he heard a scuffling on the stairway. Thinking this time it must be Mrs. Forbes, he opened the door with a gallant hello, and smiled out onto an empty landing. The square below was deserted, and there were no more footsteps to be heard. Disappointed, he was turning back to the lighted room when his boot nudged against a yielding lump. More provisions? Fetching a candle, he stooped down and discovered a dead rabbit, its body still warm and its head crushed flat, as if a wagon had run over it. Owen clung to the railing and peered into the darkness. Who would have delivered such a disgusting thing? Leaving the rabbit on the landing, he shut the door hurriedly and threw the double iron bolts.

Most doors in Roma were double-barred that night. Sunset oozed over the village like the yolk of an egg. Darkness followed swiftly, a moonless dark. Many country people took this as a warning and stayed with friends in town, waiting for daylight before trying the paths home. Children whispered from bed to bed ever wilder tales about a twelve-foot-tall blood-drinking giant who squeezed his victims into midgets, discarding them like the rinds of sucked persimmons. Behind the barred doors, hearts beat cautious as the footsteps of mice; sleepers breathed silent as feathers.

4

IN HIS LAST DREAM BEFORE WAKING, ELY SAW HIS family gathered around him, bent over his sickbed, their faces painted with worry. His sister, Caroline, chewed on the hem of the quilt that covered him, brother Ezra made monkey eyes, Pappy cried, Mammy rubbed salve on Ely's foot where it was swollen with snakebite. "Don't you worry, I'll get over this," he tried to say, "you're the ones in danger," but there was an iron weight on his tongue.

The dream left a bittersweet taste in his mind, full of remembered pain from the snakebite, and of joy in seeing his father and mother and sister still alive, before the fevers. And Ezra? Where was he?

"Where?" he cried aloud, sitting up with a jerk and staring into the murk of the lawyer's bedroom. His ankle throbbed from the old bite. More softly, he called, "Mr. Lightfoot, sir?"

Owen kept snoring. Ely shook himself and limped outside onto the landing to check the sky. And there he found the stiff rabbit. Holding it by the hind legs, he limped back inside to prod Owen in the ribs. "Mr.

Lightfoot, the sun's almost up. We've got to get a move on."

Owen snuffled and roused himself. Without spectacles or lamp he could guess by smell alone what the boy dangled from his hand. It was not the object he would have chosen to contemplate before breakfast. He propped himself up and raked the strands of hair across his scalp. "It's that beastly rabbit, isn't it?"

"Somebody must have left it for us to take along."

"So I gathered." Owen lit a candle on the bedside table. "But I felt we had quite enough provisions without *that*."

Ely hoisted the rabbit and peered at the flattened skull. "I never seen anybody kill a rabbit by stomping it."

"I thought perhaps a wagon had run over it."

"No, sir, you couldn't run over one unless it was tied down or already killed. It looks like somebody banged it with a rock." Suddenly he recalled the words of Rain Hawk, who had screamed, *Leave the rabbit for me!* He rubbed his hair. "Say, did you catch sight of the spice girl hanging around last night?"

"Mademoiselle Rozier?" said Owen. "Not that I recall." And he would have recalled, too, for he had never seen a girl whose features were more striking. Black hair, green eyes, skin the color of roasted peanuts. Mrs. Forbes was lovelier, in a conventional way, but with the frail sort of beauty one might engrave on a cameo. The spice girl's rugged beauty would be more suitable for carving in stone. "Why do you ask?"

"Oh, I was just looking for some medicine. I've got an ankle that gives me fits sometimes."

[38]

"I very much doubt whether her roots and bark would do you any good." Owen lurched from bed and wrapped a silk robe over his pajamas. "Now, perhaps you would be so good as to ask Mrs. Forbes to prepare us breakfast while I get dressed."

Ely had never known a man to wear special clothes just for sleeping. "Breakfast? Now?"

"Breakfast. It is customary to eat before one travels."

"Everybody I know," said Ely, "rides ten miles or so first, then baits the horses and feeds himself."

"We know different sorts of people." Refusing to let this young vagabond bully him, Owen insisted, "Please tell Mrs. Forbes I shall be ready in half an hour. And would you mind disposing of that bloody thing and seeing to the horses as you go?"

At the livery stable Ely tossed the rabbit to a cringing dog, then collected Babe and the lawyer's gelding, Blackstone. The word sounded Indian, but Owen had told him it was the name of an English law-writer. The horse lived up to its name, big and hard-muscled and black as obsidian. Imagine, naming such a fine animal after some blasted Englishman who wrote books! As Ely saddled up, the stableboy, Asher Gurley's nine-year-old son, stood watching him with eyes still muddy from sleep.

"You have a good hunt, Ely," the little boy mumbled.

"I'll sure try, Nathan."

The boy's eyes grew rounder. "Ely, is it true what they say about this giant fellow?"

"What is that?"

"He's an Indian ghost come to take Ohio back away from us?"

In the lantern light, Ely could not read the stable-boy's face, but he could hear the dread in his voice as clearly as he could hear the stamping of horses in the stalls. "Don't pay any mind to what folks say when they're scared. It's the war that puts all these notions in everybody's head, the war and living out here in the woods."

"They say he's a giant warrior," the boy persisted.

"I heard him called a lot of foolish things—giant and bearman and ironman—but whatever you call him he still wears breeches just like you and I do, only bigger."

"Ironman? *Iron*man!"

"Nathan, hang on a second now," Ely called as the boy's voice withdrew. "That's just a name I heard. Maybe he worked in a foundry. Nathan?" But the bare feet padded swiftly away, heading home, and Ely knew the boy's panic, heart gripped tighter and tighter, legs pumping faster, darkness whipping through his hair, feeling like a fugitive from the whole long-toothed dawn.

Ironman—what would the little ones make of that? A metal devil, bolted together, powered by steam? A mechanical soldier invented by the British to knock down our stockades? An Indian god forged by lightning? You and your big mouth, Ely Jackson.

While sunlight spilled through a crack in the horizon, he led the horses up the street, debating whether to set off by himself and just leave the pussyfoot lawyer behind to eat his breakfast and comb his hair.

Yet Ely was afraid to go alone. So he sat waiting

at Mrs. Forbes's table, tongue-tied by her outlandish looks, as she asked him in her birdsong voice about the dangers of this hunt. Would they get caught up in the war? Would they run into Indians? Dreadful animals? Quicksand? Ely had almost nerved himself to answer her with more than shrugs when the squeak of new boots and the smell of hair oil told him Owen was coming at last. The lawyer's jaw gleamed from a shave. He was wearing his courtroom getup—black suit, boiled shirt, velvet bow tie—topped off by a tall beaverskin hat.

"You planning to wear that all day on a horse?" said Ely.

"And why not?"

Ely knew better than to tamper with fools, especially grown ones from the city. Thanking Mrs. Forbes, he ate the cornmush and porkchops, even though his body was not used to eating before it had worked for two hours or so.

Owen was accustomed to eating at all hours, and ate now with gusto. Who knew what meals would be like on the road? Surely none of the cooks would be half so lovely as this one. It was a melancholy business for him to watch Mrs. Forbes glide about with her fine English posture between fireplace and table and to know that he could not take her along. Disease or savages might carry her off before he returned, or she might grow weary of this dismal village and go join her compatriots in Canada. Disease, in fact, had delivered her into Owen's life to begin with, for she had moved to Roma a year earlier as housekeeper for a minister from Boston who had soon died of typhus. Owen had immediately employed her to look after his own house and meals.

"If you've had enough," said Ely, "we ought to shake a leg."

"Of course." Owen mopped his face with the napkin. The heat was already insufferable. Turning to Mrs. Forbes, he said gravely, "Do wait for me, my dear. All of this is temporary"—he gestured beyond the greasepaper window at the cluster of hovels—"and will soon be replaced by a town suited to your character."

"How soon, Mr. Lightfoot?" she inquired, her face made up in a careful smile.

The sheriff pinned badges onto their chests and swore them in. The brand-new deputies rode away in full daylight, with most everybody outdoors to see them off. It was a town hunt, no matter if only two of them were going. The onlookers agreed that you might be able to find a boy and a man somewhere in the Ohio Valley who would make stranger partners than Ely Jackson and Owen Lightfoot, but you would have to look for a long time.

The lawyer's horse was loaded down with double saddlebags, parcels tied by thongs to the pommel, and various clinking sacks.

"You know, somebody would have to be deaf for us to sneak up on him, with you making such a racket," said Ely.

"When we draw near to our quarry, I can arrange

to be as quiet as you please," Owen replied with dignity.

Children tagged along beside the horses for a while, then one after another dropped behind. By the time they reached the spot on Bone Creek where the giant had stamped his footprints into the clay, the deputies were on their own.

"Isn't that a rather extraordinary foot?" said Owen.

The broad prints curved only slightly inward between ball and heel, as if there were no arch to the foot, and the long toes splayed outward, as if for gripping.

"I never seen anything like it before," Ely agreed.

Atop the bank, the prints showed that the giant had put on his boots again. Peering into the snarl of vines and briars and trees, unable to see more than a few yards in any direction, Owen realized the utter futility of the chase. "Now what do we do?"

Ely studied the ground without answering.

Owen scraped sweat from his forehead with a thumb. His wool suit was already clammy, and the saddle was beginning to mash his body into shapes that God had never intended. "This is preposterous. Trailing a monster through the wilderness!"

Ignoring him, Ely soon found the trail of broken weeds, the shafts bent in the direction of the bear-man's flight. "There he goes," he sang out, kicking Babe into a trot.

With a skill that seemed uncanny to Owen, Ely followed the thread of bent grass and scuffed moss for miles through the woods, until the giant's prints emerged clearly again on the Canton Road, heading south. Calling this rutted, stump-filled path a road seemed hyperbolic praise to Owen. He jolted along on Blackstone, baggage clinking, with his hat pulled down low in imitation of Ely, to guard against over-hanging branches. Sweat clung to him like fur. The suitcoat weighed on him. His legs ached as if the horse were wedging him in two.

They met a few people on the road, even a caravan of gray-bearded men and white-bonneted women trudging along like an entire seminary in migration. Ely hallooed them all, told them what he knew about the progress of the war, then asked his own questions. But no one had seen a creature answering the giant's description. And no one had seen a red-haired fellow named Ezra.

Gradually, as they rode into woods of oak and beech, the shade grew dark as cinders, the undergrowth dwindled, the roof of branches vaulted higher. Now and again Ely had to dismount, hunt in the gloom until he found a wad of damp leaves overturned, a fern bent awry, a patch of moss compacted by that huge bootprint. Then he would mount again, nod the direction, and Owen would jog behind feeling numb and blind, unable to see any of these signs until shown by Ely, and even then he could not decipher them.

For Ely the forest was written all over with signs. Pappy, who could even track Indians, had taught him how to read the woods. After learning to trail deer and wolves and raccoons, Ely thought a man was easy prey. Yet here he could not track down his own brother.

Ely had been twelve that spring when smallpox swept through the family. Pappy and Mammy and Caroline and the baby all came down with it. Why not me? Ely thought. But the fevers never lit in him or Ezra. As soon as the graves were heaped full, Ezra put him in the care of a neighbor and took off for Louisville, saying he would come fetch Ely once he found work. By the next spring there was still no word from Ezra, so Ely set out looking for him. And now, after four years of looking, he had only the rough drawing in his pocket and a headful of rumors.

At one of the stops for watering the horses, Owen dug some blackberry pie out of a saddlebag. Ely would not have any, so the lawyer ate it all himself. Nor would Ely accept any brandy from the silver flask Owen held out to him.

"I don't believe in it," Ely said, shutting his lips tight.

"What is there to believe in?"

"I do how I do, and you do how you do."

"Is it a religious scruple, if you don't mind my asking?" Owen retained enough of his own Quaker scruples to feel guilty about his drinking, but not enough to make him give it up.

"I don't need religion to tell me drink can ruin a man."

"Indeed it can, if used immoderately," Owen agreed, screwing the cap onto the flask.

There was nothing furtive about the trail they followed the rest of that day. After leaving the creek the bearman had simply plodded on at that ground-eating pace of his, avoiding farms and villages. Headed south for the Ohio, Ely guessed, and that would carry him to the Mississippi, then to the Gulf of Mexico, and then to anywhere on earth. Nobody leaves tracks on water. But if the bearman moved in daylight, people would remember him.

Every jostling pace drove the wedge of pain deeper into Owen's spine, until he could barely keep from crying out. He was reminded of slogging to Pittsburgh across the Alleghenies. It was no wonder those wretched mountains were called the "backbone of America," for they had doubtless ruined many a spine. He suspected the reason so few people ever moved back East from Ohio was because they recalled the misery of traveling out.

The bearman's path conceded nothing to the rough country, leading them along hogback ridges, up ravines, through canes that grew as close and hard as ribs. Occasionally the deputies heard barking dogs or thudding axes, yet the trail rarely brought them within sight of people. At one point, where the bearman had leaped twenty feet or more across a river, there were handprints in the clay: broad as skillets, but without claws, and without those webs between the fingers that some of the old-timers back in Roma had predicted. Plain old human hands, thought Ely.

As the sun drooped onto the spires of cedars, Owen inquired numbly, "Where do you suppose he slept that first night?"

"Nowhere we've got to yet," answered Ely, who had caught the bearman's fierceness, and would stop for nothing but dark.

It was nearly dark when they came to a homestead. The trees had been girdled and stood gaunt, leafless, about the cabin. A measly stand of corn grew among the scarred trunks. The cabin door hung crookedly open, like a broken jaw, and the giant's path led straight to it. The deputies kept their distance, watching that crippled doorway, for even if the giant himself wasn't hiding there, some homesteader might be, and might shoot anybody rash enough to saunter up to his cabin at sunset.

The woods were hushed—no birds calling, no crickets or locusts, no frogs. Because of us? Ely wondered, or because he's denned up in that cabin? He drew the flintlock from its sling, dropped the mare's reins, and leaped to the ground. "I'm going to have a look," he whispered to Owen. "If anything stirs, fire in the air. Don't aim to hit anything, just make a noise."

"Why not wait for daylight?" Owen hissed in reply.

Ely was already creeping toward the cabin, thinking, I'm not ready to meet him yet, don't know enough about him. But if he's here, he's here. The door hung awry by two leather hinges. Ely crawled up beside the black opening and crouched there, listening. No sound at all, as if the earth were padded in wool. But there was a powerful stink, sour and nose-burning. Would the bearman come just this far, thinking to hole up here until the murder was forgotten? In the failing light, the sun gone down below the rim of woods, Ely could see no path of broken weeds leading away from the cabin.

Ely Jackson, he thought, you got the guts of an angel. Go ahead, he told himself, forcing his head past the doorframe and staring into the cabin. He could see nothing, might have been staring into the blackness of a throat. And he knew his own skull would stand out against the sky like an iron target.

Boom! a gun went off, and Ely slumped to the ground. Where is he? Where? A second later Owen's voice rose plaintively from the woods: "I'm terribly sorry. I must have been holding the trigger too firmly."

Ely sprawled for a minute on his belly, panting, before he could speak. His heart was a wreck. Why had he ever agreed to travel with this sack of guts? "You mean you didn't see anything move?" he called out at last.

"Fortunately not."

The lawyer was about as much use as a hound that barked at shadows. "Well, bring a candle," Ely shouted.

"Of course, of course."

Owen's face was a fat moon as he sidled up to Ely bearing a candle through the ghostly trees. In the flickering light they could see the marks of violence more clearly—the door planking burst from its crossbrace, two hinges torn from the jamb.

"The latchstring was out," Ely said, "and he didn't know to tug on it. He just slammed his way through like a bull."

"I hope whoever lives here was away from home," said Owen.

Shoving against his fear, Ely stepped inside, raising the candle so as to shed light on all four corners of the room. Owen stole in after him, drawn like a moth to the candle's pale flicker. There was a rope bed against the rear wall, a blanket chest beside it, and in the center a puncheon table. From wall pegs hung a stool, a wooden bowl, an ax, half a dozen pelts on stretchers. It was a bachelor place. It could have been Ely's own cabin, and that made him feel queer.

"What a stench," Owen whispered.

"About like rats rotted under the corncrib," said Ely.

"Do you suppose he was just looking for a place to sleep?"

"Food, more likely." Stooping beside the hearth, Ely felt the ashes. Cold. He lifted the candle above a crock filled with lard, and saw inside the marks where thick fingers had raked through the fat. Next to it was a potato sack that had been ripped open. Scattered on the floor were gristly sprouts, partly gnawed potatoes, and the bloody remains of a possum.

Light or no light, Owen turned away and hastened outside to breathe some pure air. Added to the stench and the day's jouncing ride, the thought of swallowing lard and raw opossum turned his stomach. "Shouldn't we be finding someplace to camp?"

"Directly." Ely lingered, half wanting to sleep on the rope bed with its mattress of leaves, where the bearman must have slept, in order to feel his way closer to the big man, to be readier next time for meeting him.

"Aren't you coming?" Owen called in a strained voice.

At last Ely retreated, carrying the candle toward the horses.

They built a fire and sat facing away from it into the night. Ely cradled his flute. Owen spread the traveling desk onto his lap but could not think of a word to write. When did Lewis and Clark compose their journals? Where did they find the energy, let alone the inspiration, after a day on the trail? This first day of the hunt had left him so bruised that he could not imagine suffering through another mile of it. But how could he confess defeat so quickly to this backwoods boy, who already held him in such contempt?

Ely was too wrought-up by the chase to play his flute. Staring into the dark, he felt the earth alive beneath him, the earth like an immense beast covered by a fur of trees and here and there a tiny human clearing like a sore where the hair had been rubbed away. He thought about the spice girl, figuring she must have been the one who left that mangled rabbit, wondering what she meant by it. And he thought about the bearman, who would be bedded down somewhere further west, deeper into the woods.

5

WHATEVER QUALMS OWEN HAD FELT AT THE outset of the chase regarding his moody young partner were amply confirmed on the following days. The boy was possessed. He would not stop for meals, would not stop at night before pitch darkness. So long as he could see well enough to discover those boot-prints, or could find settlers who had glimpsed the big man lumbering down the trails, Ely kept on riding, and Owen felt compelled to follow. Nonetheless, since one stretch of woods looked very much like another to him, Owen could not help asking: "Are you quite sure you know where we are?"

"Yes, sir," Ely answered, "I been all through this country hunting for my brother."

Owen refrained from asking how the brother had become lost, figuring this prickly boy would speak only when he was ready.

Each night they built a fire, despite the muggy weather, to discourage mosquitoes and to have some-thing besides one another to stare at. Ely played his flute and brooded on the bearman. Owen sat near the flames reading Gibbon or penning a few weary lines in his journal.

"What is that you're scribbling?" Ely asked him one time.

"My reflections on our day's journey."

"What is there to say about it?"

This exchange led Owen to suspect that Ely could neither read nor write—a suspicion later confirmed when the boy gazed at the spine of his book and asked, "What is that you keep reading every night?"

"An account of how the Roman Empire succumbed to barbarism," Owen explained.

Whereupon Ely said, "Who gives a dang about dead Romans?"

On the fifth day, just when Owen felt they must have reached the limits of the habitable globe, they arrived at a village.

"This whole territory sure is filling up," Ely said. "When I come through here two years ago this wasn't nothing but woods."

"It's not much of an improvement on the forest, if you ask me," said Owen.

At least the village possessed a blacksmith, who attended to the horses' shoes, and a tavern where Owen hoped to enjoy a hot supper and a bed. The sign out front displayed a white-clad maiden with torch uplifted and the words GODDESS OF LIBERTY. The air inside was murky with tobacco smoke. Teamsters, whose wagons were loaded with supplies for the northern armies, played cards at tables while dogs crawled about their feet gobbling scraps of food. The innkeeper sat near the fireplace, a half-plucked chicken dangling from one fist, a ruff of stray feathers adhering to his beard.

Ely asked the usual questions, first about his brother and then about the giant.

"He came through here, all right," the innkeeper said. "I never saw anything to beat him. He was great big—eight foot high, I figure—and broad as a wagon bed. He had a black beard, silvery at the tips, growing high on his cheeks almost up to his eyes. There was hair pretty much everywhere you could see—back of his hands, his throat, on his chest where the shirt was open. His eyes were yellow and glassy, like if you ever looked at a cat's eyes."

"You're sure it was a man?" Ely asked.

"What else could he be?" Scraps of firelight washed over the innkeeper's face. Card games paused as the teamsters waited to hear what he would say. "I mean, he walked on his hind legs."

"Did he cause any trouble?" Owen said.

"We didn't give him the chance. Symmes here"—he pointed to one of the card players—"rode in yesterday noon saying there was a giant coming down the Canton Road. 'Giant?' we said. But such godawful things have passed through here lately, with the war and all, we had to believe him. So a bunch of us went up the road to have a look. And sure enough, here come this great big bruiser. 'What you want?' we yelled. He paid us no mind, just kept on coming. We yelled louder, but he never slowed up. We figured we'd have to shoot him to stop him. Then five yards away he pulls up and begins to signing with his fingers like an Indian."

They had figured out he wanted to work in exchange for food. While they stood around him with guns, the giant split a cord of wood and dug manure into the innkeeper's garden, after which he ate a ham and twenty eggs and drank a gallon of cider. Since nobody wanted him to sleep nearby, at sundown they escorted him from the village. Before leaving, he spoke to them again with his hands. A trapper who knew Indian sign said the giant was asking how to find a cave on the beautiful river, from which everybody figured he must be looking for the bluffs on the Ohio west of Cincinnati.

"Since he couldn't understand what we told him," the innkeeper said, staring into the fireplace where spitted chickens dripped fat, "my wife wrote the directions on a patch of leather and pinned it to his shirt. That way, if he gets lost, he can always have somebody read his tag."

"Where did you send him first?" said Ely. "To Coshocton?"

The innkeeper peeled a white feather from his tongue. "There, and then to Zanesville, down the Muskingum to Marietta, then on down the Ohio to wherever it is he's looking for."

The very names deepened Owen's fatigue. Despite the filthy condition of the tavern, the dogs groveling beneath the tables, and the odor of singed feathers, he was quite looking forward to a night indoors. As he was about to ask the host for lodging, however, he observed his partner making for the door.

"Wherever can you be going at this hour?" Owen said.

"To Coshocton."

Having learned that it was no use arguing with Ely once his mind was made up, Owen accompanied him to the blacksmith's, where they retrieved the horses. "We're gaining on him," Ely called exuberantly, swinging into the saddle. Owen mounted with a good deal less enthusiasm, since his buttocks felt as though he had spent the last five days straddling a lighted stove.

The giant had walked to Coshocton, hitched aboard a wagon to Zanesville, then worked his way on a keelboat down the Muskingum toward Marietta, leaving a trail of rumors behind him like the fiery tail behind a comet.

The deputies could form no clear picture from the scraps of stories they heard along the giant's path: the tales of sheep torn apart, not the way a wolf would do it, by teeth and claws, but limb from limb; the woman whose husband had come home to find her sitting numb and hollow-eyed on the table, and could get no words out of her except *huge hands*; the family who had watched in amazement while the enormous stranger set their mired wagon back upon the road; a child trapped by rains at a ford, carried on the big man's shoulders through rapids to safety; another child run off three times, telling each time he was brought back that the wild man had called him from the woods; bear-hunting dogs that scrambled yapping into the darkness and never returned; wood split, calves delivered, barns cleaned overnight where the giant had slept; two women in different counties whose faces had taken on the same dreaminess when asked about the ironman; farmers who had shot at him as he stood at the edge of a field, others who had taken him home to dinner after a morning of shared hoeing.

The deputies could no longer be sure which of the stories truly belonged to the bearman, and which had been hung on him by amazed or frightened people for want of any other hook. Anything might be blamed on the hulking, silent man: a tree uprooted, a pie stolen, a horse lamed, a rail fence torn down.

Rather than take a boat from Coshocton to Marietta, as the ironman had done, Ely thought to save time by riding overland, cutting off a great loop of the river. The only path turned out to be an old buffalo trace overgrown with brush.

Holding an arm across his face to ward off branches as the horses plowed on, Owen said, "There must be an easier route."

"We'll get there, Mr. Lightfoot, don't you worry," said Ely.

"Are you certain you know this territory?"

"There's a stretch here and there I never been to before."

"Would my compass be of any service?"

Ely turned in the saddle and gave him an incredulous stare. "How's your compass going to know where Marietta's at?"

Owen knew better than to bicker with Ely when he had that shine in his eyes. There was a sense of gathered force in him, like a dog poised to attack or run. Despite the deerskin clothes and backwoods manners and unlettered speech, here was a youth to be taken seriously. He seemed to Owen like an ax, lean and sharp, beating his way by force of will through every obstacle.

Lewis and Clark must be such men, Owen imagined. How else could they have sliced through ten thousand miles of troubles and miseries? Thinking of the great explorers, who carved their names in trees and cliffs on their journey to the Pacific, Owen carved his own name into the gray trunk of a beech at the next watering stop. He still yearned to collect specimens, as Lewis and Clark had done. Grizzly bears! Buffalo! Yet when he gazed at the wild sprawl of vegetation, he had no idea which plants were remarkable and which were quite ordinary; nor could he shoot well enough to kill any of the beasts that he and Ely scared up. So he jogged along, his case of instruments unopened, his collecting boxes empty.

Toward evening on the eighth day, clouds thickened for a storm. While Owen fed corn to the horses and tied their hobbles, Ely evicted a clan of foxes from the hollow bole of a sycamore.

"There's room inside here for both of us," he told Owen.

"That's quite all right. I'll make do with my umbrella."

"Suit yourself. Leastways, hand me in your books and that box of telescopes and such. No sense in spoiling them." Ely stowed these inside the tree, then added: "My saddle blanket's so full of grease it don't scarcely leak at all, if you want to throw that around you."

"No, no, thank you very much." As the first rain spattered down, Owen unfurled his umbrella and shut his eyes. He was trying to imagine what could possibly induce him to spend the night in a fox's den inside a hollow tree, when a burst of wind shattered the ribs of his umbrella, slashing him with rain, and he had his answer. "I say, are you quite sure there's room?"

"Come on," said Ely, drawing him in by the arm, "before you turn into a muskrat."

Small bones on the floor of the cavity snapped beneath Owen's hands and knees as he crawled inside. The air was pungent with the smell of foxes and rotting wood. Rain smoked down and thunder shook the ground and lightning sizzled in the treetops.

Shouting to make himself heard, Ely observed, "It's a regular goose-drowner."

Owen sat with feet drawn up, arms hugging his knees, and listened to the onslaught. It was impossible to believe that nature worked without malice. How could blind forces have contrived a medium more foul for tramping through than this clinging mud, more foul for breathing than this sodden air? And what of the cabins snatched away by flooded rivers, corn burned crisp by sun, fields reclaimed by scrub, children fetched off by fever, cattle poisoned by snakes, men drawn by the lure of distant grasses, women seduced by Indians? How could you build a civilization in the face of such elemental hostility?

"By Jesus, I do love a hard rain!" cried Ely, who always grew tender and confessional during storms.

"Frankly, they terrify me," said Owen.

"The reason I love them is because when I was just little and it would come up a thunderstorm, my pappy used to wrap me in a blanket and carry me onto the porch and we'd watch it together, and there'd be mist on my face and the thunder going right up my backbone. Sometimes he'd sing, his chest rumbling against me, or tell me stories about when he was a boy in the mountains. Other times he'd just keep quiet."

There was a lull in the thunder. As if he could not speak except under cover of the storm's racket, Ely fell silent. In the stillness, Owen heard for the first time a faint chattering and the shifting of tiny bodies in the darkness overhead.

Sensing the sharp upward tilt of Owen's head, Ely said, "It's just bats. Don't mind them. When this rain lets up, they'll be going out to hunt. Keep back away from the hole and they won't smack into you."

Even as he finished speaking, the dark shapes began to appear, darting in and out, silhouetted against the patch of twilight visible through the opening at the base of the tree. Owen squeezed himself against the opposite wall of the cavity, scarcely able to breathe. Among the few occasions on which his father had ever shown anger was when bats would flutter down the chimney, and the Quaker gentleman would swat them with a rug-beater, pick up their stunned bodies with fire tongs, and drop them into the stove. Owen could not recall ever having been swaddled in a blanket and carried anywhere by his father. Shutting his eyes, so as not to see the bats, he said, "Your father sounds like an excellent parent."

"Pappy? Oh, when he was around, he was a good one. Fed us, taught us hunting, never beat us. But he didn't stick around too much of the time. He was what you'd call a mover, always looking for cheaper land somewhere, or fewer people, or dirt that would raise crops without you working it. Every time we'd get a patch cleared and a cabin thrown up, he'd get itchy feet and light out, come back maybe six months later for the rest of us. And we'd stay in the new place a season or two, then off he'd go. I lived all over Tennessee and Kentucky that way."

"Six months? Would he be searching for land all that time?"

"Mostly he was just rambling, I figure, living like a bachelor again, camping in the woods, killing Indians."

The casual way in which Ely reported this came as a shock to Owen. "Killing Indians? Whatever for?"

"Sometimes to save his own skin. But most often, the way he told it, he was just cleaning them out of the woods, making room for white people to settle. To tell you the honest truth, I think he liked killing. It was the only thing he was good at, and he'd brag about it every chance he got."

"Why, that's monstrous."

"I reckon so. But how do you figure we can sit here safe and snug in Ohio and not an Indian village within a day's walk?"

"Because of treaties," Owen insisted.

Ely laughed uproariously. "Is that what they say in Philadelphia? Treaties? Money paid down fair and square to whatever drunk chiefs they can round up, and General Wayne's army there just to act as witnesses? No, sir, Mr. Lightfoot, what cleared this territory was gunpowder and lead."

The rain hissed down with renewed violence, and the air inside the tree suddenly thickened with an inrush of bats. Owen held his breath as the flimsy wings grazed his cheeks. Oblivious to the bats, soothed by the downpour, Ely went on: "Anyhow, that's what Pappy always said. Gunpowder and lead. He'd ride all the way down into Georgia to hunt Cherokee. It's a wonder they never trailed him home and chopped us all to pieces. That's what I kept fearing—one day he'd come riding hard for the cabin with a whole pack of yelling Cherokee on his tail. But that wasn't what killed him." Ely stopped abruptly, as if he had discovered himself one step away from a cliff's edge.

"What did kill him?"

The darkness and the rain enabled Ely to speak of his deepest hurt. "Same thing as killed my sister and mammy and baby brother. Smallpox. Pappy come down with it first, maybe carried it back with him from his last raid. By the time me and Ezra buried him, Mammy was too feverish to get up out of bed and say prayers over him. We buried Caroline next, then Mammy, then little Moses. Me and Ezra hung around the cabin for days and days, waiting to die. But we never got sick. Then one morning Ezra handed me over to a neighbor lady, said he was going to look for work in Louisville and he'd come fetch me as soon as he was all fixed up. And that was the last I seen of him."

Owen pictured the lone cabin, the humped graves, the two boys waiting for their own deaths. "And so you've been searching for him ever since?"

"Right at four years now. I'll go months without finding any trace of him, and then I'll say his name in some stable or tavern, and people will remember this redheaded guy who fixed a roof or built a cupboard or sold them a pair of beaverskins."

"And the rumors eventually led you to Roma?"

"Last May. A shopkeeper in Chillicothe said he'd paid Ezra to drive a load of blankets to Cleveland. Ezra left Chillicothe in the wagon, but the last place anybody saw him driving it was in Roma."

"And since then you've found no further trace of him?"

"Not yet. But I ain't through looking by a long shot."

"Are you bitter at him for leaving you?"

Ely pondered that while the bats stirred on their roost and the rain smoked down. Then he said quietly, "I used to think I'd yell at him and carry on if I ever caught up with him. I had speeches all worked out, just what I'd say. Why'd he run off and leave me, and him the only blood I've got on earth? But I got to thinking. He's Pappy's boy, just like me. And we both caught the same itch for moving on. Wouldn't I have done the same, if I was the older brother?"

"But what of your father's pleasure in killing? At least you didn't catch that from him."

"I hope not," said Ely thoughtfully. "Lord, I hope not."

In the silence following the storm, Ely felt ashamed for having spoken so openly of himself. Never lay yourself open. Had Pappy felt this way after a drinking spell, ashamed of telling heart secrets to strangers? An arm's length away, Owen's face shone like foxfire. What's he thinking about me? Ely wondered. Is he nailing me to the walls of his mind with fifty-cent words?

6

ALL NIGHT, AS BATS FLUTTERED IN TO FEED AT THEIR roosts in the hollow of the tree, a rain of insect parts sifted down on the sleeping deputies, the heads of fireflies and legs of beetles and the dusty wings of moths. When he awoke, Owen could not identify the summery taste on his tongue. After sleeping all night curled like a fetus, he unbent painfully. He drew the spectacles from his vest, wiped them on the greasy tail of his shirt, then peered through them at the gray, dripping dawn. Shirt, spectacles, skin, everything about him was filthy from nine days of travel.

Ely stirred in his sleep. Suddenly he cried out and began flailing his arms, pounding Owen, slapping the walls of the tree.

Owen clutched his head to ward off the blows. "Wake up, Ely, wake up!"

Coming to himself, Ely opened his eyes and saw the huge bear-shaped demon of his nightmare transformed into this fat lawyer. "Oh, Mr. Lightfoot, I was dreaming you were him."

"Who?"

"Him. The giant." Ely brushed the insect grit from his hair. Finding a grasshopper, he popped it into his mouth.

Owen blinked. "Did you *eat* that?"

"You want one?" Ely cupped another grasshopper in his palm and offered it to the lawyer, who drew back as if it were a knife thrust at him. "Not your kind of breakfast?" Ely curled his lip and ate the grass-hopper. "I keep forgetting you're a city man. Bet you're sorry you ever come along with a roughneck like me."

"Not at all, not at all," Owen protested.

"We was raised different, I guess."

"Yes, indeed. As different as night and day."

Ely felt a quick flare of anger. "Does that make you better than me? Does that give you call to think I'm backward? Dumb and low and poor as the dirt?" Before Owen could answer, Ely crawled from the tree into the morning drizzle.

Later, riding along the mired path that stretched away before them like a smear of poisonous custard, Owen still felt dazed by this exchange. He could not for the life of him think what had provoked the boy. They traveled in silence, gnawing apples and biscuits and day-old turkey legs for breakfast. The horses gleamed. The sky was the color of gunpowder.

Ely was surprised by his own anger. Why should he care what some high-and-mighty lawyer thought of him? He glanced at Owen. The store-bought suit had begun to sag. The white shirt had grown as dingy as a slate floor. Rain gathered on the hat brim, which drooped above Owen's jowly face like a collapsed roof on a barn. City man, head full of books, looking down his nose at me. Out loud, Ely said, "Just because my pappy killed Indians and drank whiskey, don't you think he was the scum of the earth. And don't you think Ezra hates me just because he run off and left me."

Taken aback, Owen stammered, "I'm sure I wasn't thinking anything of the sort."

"I don't have to apologize to nobody."

Their two horses trotted along broadside to one another, like ships squared off for battle. Owen twisted in his saddle. "If there is something you'd like to explain—"

"We got a job to do together, but that don't mean I have to explain myself to you."

"Talking over a problem like reasonable—"

"Talk talk talk! I'm fed up with talk! What I want is quiet!" Reaching over and seizing Blackstone's reins, Ely jerked both horses to a halt. In a voice that was also reined in, restraining his fury, he said, "I'm thinking we ought to split up. I'll keep on after the giant. You do what you like."

Owen drew himself erect in the saddle. The stillness in the boy's face made him cautious. "Would it give you satisfaction to have me quit now and run home with my tail between my legs?"

"It ain't a matter of my satisfaction."

"Then what *is* the matter?"

His eyes burning with sudden, astonishing tears, Ely said, "I was glad you come along with me because you know the law, you know what's right and what's not right when you go to hunting a man. I didn't figure you'd be mocking me."

"When have I mocked you?"

"It's how you look at me and talk to me, how you go scratching in your journal and reading in your book every night."

"But that's ridiculous," Owen protested. "I never meant—"

"Can I help it I don't know how to read? Can I help it I don't know a thing in the world but woods and dirt and beasts?"

"You've mistaken me completely, I assure you."

"Maybe." Releasing Blackstone's bridle, Ely wrapped the blanket around his shoulders against the rain, the same blanket in which he had wrapped the dwarf. His eyes burned. "Well, you coming with me, or you turning back?"

"I'm coming with you," said Owen decisively.

Heeling Babe in the ribs, Ely set off toward the Muskingum. Mud clung to the horses' hooves, letting go with a sucking sound. The rain quit by noon, and the sky turned china-blue. Closer to the river, the buffalo trace began to show signs of care. Stumps had been pulled, brush cleared, ruts filled with gravel. The deputies soon came to a settlement where men were building a stockade fence. When Ely asked them what it was for, they said the Shawnee and Miami had raided upriver two nights before, and the British were rumored to be on the march from Detroit.

"Shawnee and Miami?" Ely objected. "They're peaceable."

"They ain't anymore."

Reaching the Muskingum, whose waters ran surly brown from the rain, the deputies rode through one fortified village after another, and in each one the story was the same. Indians were prowling. The British were coming. They met men laboring along the towpath, dragging keelboats upriver by ropes. No, the boatmen declared, raising their eyebrows at Ely's description, they hadn't seen any giant and didn't care to.

When the road swerved inland to avoid a cluster of rotting cabins, the deputies kept near the river, to find out whether anyone in this tumbledown place had caught sight of the bearman. What had once been the main street was overgrown with sumac and sassafras and blackberry. The far end of the street cut a notch in the horizon, like the sight on a gun.

Owen surveyed the ruins. "What doom came over this place?"

"It could have been a flood," Ely suggested, "or sickness, or a bad winter. Who knows? Could have been a hundred things." On his travels he had seen such villages before, husks abandoned like snakeskin. Disease or dread would scare people off, and then evil reputation would keep anyone new from settling there.

They rode slowly between the decaying cabins. Moss grew on the bark roofs. The plank sidewalks had been split by saplings and bleached gray by weather. In the windows of a log church a few panes of glass still glinted, and an iron cross tilted from the steeple. Town bones, thought Ely. He sat with one hand on the butt of his rifle, sniffing the air. "There's powerful bad medicine in this place, if nobody's stole that window glass."

"Indeed," said Owen. He shifted uneasily in the saddle. "Hadn't we ought to make our way to Marietta before dark?"

"Shoosh. Listen at that." From nearby came a sound like the rasp of a dry pump. In a swift movement Ely tugged the rifle from its sling and swung the muzzle toward the noise.

Out of a bramble patch near the horses' feet limped a gaunt hound, its muzzle thrust at the sky and its jaws open as if it were howling. But it produced only a faint wheeze.

"Lost its voice," Ely said. "Howled it away."

"Can they *do* that?"

"If they're scared or mad enough. I've seen them do it chasing bears." The hound's ribs heaved from the effort of its hoarse barking. Ely winced at the sound. "Something sure scared the tar and gizzard out of this one."

Hesitantly, Owen asked, "Could it have been our friend the giant, do you think?"

Instead of answering, Ely gazed from cabin to cabin, hunting for signs of the big man. Most doorways stood open onto black windowless interiors, the hinges and locks eaten away by rust. Can I face into fifteen more pitch-black holes? he wondered.

"Wouldn't the dog have run away if the giant were nearby?" Owen said.

"Not if he thought he had the big fellow treed in one of these cabins. He'd skulk around baying at the door until his voice was gone." Ely chucked the reins against the mare's neck. "Let's go see."

As they rode forward, the dog retreated before them

with a hobbling gait, one hind leg dragging, muzzle lifted and gaping.

"Something's broke its leg," Ely said. Passing near the rotting cabins, he smelled only dirt, wood, rusty iron.

The hound kept backing away until it reached a stone house by the river. The building must once have been a grand sight—three stories high, slate roof, walls as stout as a fortress—but now vines fingered through gaps in the stone, flowers sprouted on the window ledges, bushes grew from what was left of the roof. The river had undercut one corner of the foundation, and the house had begun to settle crookedly. All that remained of the wharf were a few pilings, thrust above the river like decayed teeth.

Out front of this forsaken mansion the dog hunkered down, legs quivering, muzzle on paws. There were claw marks on the door at a dog's height.

Ely smelled man—the rancid, festering odor of sweat-soaked bedding and rotted food. "There's somebody here."

Thinking, now's my chance to show the boy, Owen slid hastily down. "My turn to investigate," he said, and went creeping toward the door, rifle thrust forward as if it were a pitchfork.

It's all a bluff, Ely thought, to prove he's as brave or foolish as me. But his chickenheart will stop him directly. To Ely's amazement, however, Owen stole right up to the door and shoved it open with his gun barrel. Inside, someone stood in front of a lamp, one arm raised, a looming shape. Owen gave a cry, jumped aside, flung himself against the outer wall.

"You come on out here!" Ely shouted, his rifle aimed at the menacing silhouette.

The shape dwindled as it neared the daylight. Out walked a small man as haggard and ancient as the hound, as dilapidated as the village. The lines of his face reminded Ely of Rain Hawk. Part Shawnee? Bells on his ankles jingled with each step. His lifted palm glowed red in the sun. "Peace to you, brothers," he declared solemnly.

"What are you doing here?" Ely demanded.

"This is my place." He wore a ratty swallowtail coat and trousers shiny from age, what must once have been a stiff white collar around his neck, and on his head a gray judge's wig, with two feathers stuck in a headband. The wasted eyes gazed squarely at Ely. "You are a missionary, Red-Hair?"

"No," said Ely.

"You have come to kill me?"

"Lands, no. Where'd you get such a notion?"

"Then put away your gun. I give you no call to use it." The old man waved his hand sideways, as one shoos a fly.

Ely rested the flintlock across the saddle, but did not return it to the sling. "Are you alone here?"

"There is also my dog."

"Nobody else?"

The old man spread his arms wide, then let them fall to his side in a gesture of immense weariness. "As you see, the place is cursed. There is no one else."

"Did a great big man pass through here yesterday, black hair all over him, maybe a patch of leather pinned on his chest?"

The old man raised his eyebrows. "You have seen the dog."

"It tangled with the giant?"

"It is a very foolish dog." Bells jingled and feathers waggled as the old man shifted his feet.

Still breathing hard, Owen asked, "Did it chase him away?"

The old man did not smile—there was not enough slack in his face for that—but the line of his mouth softened and the creases near his eyes deepened. "The great one does not run away."

"Where'd he go when he left here?" Ely asked.

The sun seemed to glow in the old man's face. The eyes were netted with burst veins. "The river took him."

"Took him where? Did he ask directions?"

"He was seeking a burial place of the Old People."

"Some kind of cave on the Ohio?" said Ely.

The old man nodded gravely. "On the beautiful river, yes."

"How did he speak to you?" Owen asked.

The old man stretched forward his two cupped hands in a pantomime of giving. "I gave him bread."

Owen persisted. "Did he speak English?"

"He brought the dog to me." The old man curled his arms in a cradling gesture. The sleeves fell away, revealing wrists as tough and thin as ax handles. Every phrase now was accompanied by pantomime, as if he spoke to the deaf. "He was sad, because he had broken the dog's leg. There was gentleness in him, but he did not understand his strength." A grimace crossed the old man's face, and then the calm returned. "Why do you hunt him?"

Because I have to see the creature who made those tracks, Ely thought, but said only, "We think he killed a man up north."

"Killing!" The old man spat. The skin was stretched taut on the frame of his face. There was Indian blood in him, Ely could tell. It showed in the bones. About the same mix of white and red as in the spice girl. "Who are you to speak of killing? Look around you." The sweep of the old man's arms took in the desolate village. "This is your work, the death of my people."

"Old one," said Ely, "we never hurt your people or anybody. We want to stop the murdering. That's why we're on this hunt."

"Your missionaries also came to us preaching peace, with their hats like the wings of crows and their holy book." The voice wavered with age and anger, but kept on until the bitter tale was finished: "In time we heard their words. We gave up war. We buried the stone of war, and only the elders knew where it was. We built a white man's village. With axes we smoothed logs and split shingles for the roofs. We piled stones for this mission house here by the river. So we lived many seasons. But your people crowded us. They filled the woods until the air was thick with their sounds. Our brothers who still made war moved to where the sun sets, but we stayed here, trusting in the god Jesus." All the while his ax-handle arms spoke the words in gestures.

"Then one day when I was a boy your men came

on horses to stand where your horses stand now. They called us out to speak to them, and the father said go, my children, they will not harm you. But I climbed into the loft of this house and hid, for I was afraid of the white men. They led my people one by one into this house and killed them with clubs. I watched from the loft. My people did not fight, because the god Jesus taught us never to fight. A few ran away into the woods, but they grew old and died. I am the only one left in this place. No one stops here, because they do not want to hear what I have to say."

In the steep sunlight, the old man's eyes were blank with shadow, like the windows in the gutted cabins. Ely looked away at the slick brown current of the Muskingum, thinking of Pappy's stories about hunting Indians. He felt a bone-deep sadness.

"Do not come to me with talk of killing," said the old man. "Let the great one go."

Owen roused himself. "We can't do that. We can't just let murderers go. Somewhere there must be a stop."

"And will you hang him?" The old man squeezed his hands, stringy with veins, about his own neck. He peered from Owen to Ely, then dropped his arms. "Is not hanging still more killing?"

Nettled by this, Owen said, "How did he converse with you?"

"He spoke only with his hands." The old man thrust his palms forward. "As I have spoken to you, even though you have no eyes to see."

"Your hands say you will never forgive us," Ely told him.

A look of mild surprise swept over the taut skin of his face, like wind across water. "You watch well, Red-Hair. You have eyes. The father said the god Jesus wants us to forgive evil, but I say no. The god Jesus has lost his power."

Owen stood up. Startled, the dog lurched to its feet and resumed its scratchy howling.

"Do not follow him." The bells jingled as the old man stepped near and put a hand on Babe's neck. "He is not bound by our law. He is not one of us."

"What do you mean?" said Ely.

"He is another kind of two-legged. My people call him Omee, the bearman who walks in the night. He must be left alone."

"What's a bearman?" Ely demanded. If this old half-breed and Rain Hawk had the same name for him, maybe the giant wasn't human after all.

The feathered head waggled from side to side. "Let him go."

Owen climbed onto Blackstone. Babe danced a few steps sideways under Ely. Neither deputy made a move to ride away.

At length, Ely said, "I wish we could have lived in peace."

The old man touched Ely's knee. "You must not forget what I have told you. When I die, there will be no memory in this place. Your people will come here and cover our land with their own stories."

For most of the way to Marietta, the deputies did not speak. Each turned the old man's tale over and over in his mind, as if it were a mysterious pebble.

On the outskirts of Marietta they came upon a gang

of children tormenting a broken-winged hawk with sticks and rocks.

"You kids quit that!" Ely yelled. "Shoo! Get!" Leaping down, he killed the hawk with the butt of his rifle.

Owen stared at the mud-spattered wings, the savage beak. "I won't run, I won't turn back," he said with determination, as if Ely had challenged him again.

7

IN MARIETTA THEY LEARNED THAT THE GIANT, WITH a tag still pinned to his chest, had hired on to a keelboat bound for Cincinnati. The deputies found passage in a boat that was lashed together with six others, all filled with settlers and livestock. People clambered from boat to boat, swapping food and talk. One vessel was devoted to cooking, another to preaching, and a third to music. In the daytime, Ely dangled a hook for catfish and perch, while Owen sought out a quiet corner to read Gibbon and to write in his journal. At night, Ely divided his time between the music boat, where he played his flute and danced on his hands to the fiddling, and the preaching boat, where he listened to sermons with the same rapt attention he paid to thunderstorms.

"I hadn't realized you were religiously inclined," Owen remarked to him one evening.

"I been dipped in religion a few times, but it don't stick."

Thinking of his own Quaker parents, their sober bearing, their black garb, their pregnant silences, Owen asked, "Were your mother and father devout in their beliefs?"

Ely gave him a sharp look, on the watch for mockery. Not sensing any, he replied, "Mammy could read a little in the Bible. Kept saying she'd teach me, and never did. And Pappy'd catch religion every spring when the revivalists come through. For a while he'd speak in tongues and dance on the pews and groan about his sinful nature, but pretty soon he'd get over it. He was the sort of Christian who'd bless the whole pig when he slaughtered it, and that blessing would do until the last of it was eaten."

Neither pork nor any other food appealed to Owen so long as he remained afloat. Yet the river was mercifully calm, pouring westward at the speed of a man's walk. For a week it carried them past farms, towns, coal pits, salt works, mills. At dusk, limbs overhanging the water bent low under the weight of roosting pigeons. Deer grazed in meadows along the banks, lifting their narrow muzzles to gaze at the passing boats. Willows trailed thin branches in the current like women washing their hair. Canebrakes lined the shore, and grapevines snarled the treetops. Fiery orange and gold parakeets flitted among the dark hemlocks. Unlike the warblers that sang outside his cabin on the morning Ely discovered the dwarf, these birds knew what season it was and held their peace, perched among the green boughs like ornaments.

Whenever they passed a major river—the Kanawha, Big Sandy, Scioto—one or two boats cut free, delivering settlers to their land. By the sixth day, the boat in which the deputies rode was drifting alone.

Since the river was high, the owner—a merchant anxious to beat a rival to Cincinnati with a load of stoves—decided they would float all night. He studied his *Navigator* by lamplight, peering over the dark water in search of landmarks. Ely and Owen squinted into the gloom, on the watch for sandbars and snags and the bristling humped backs of islands. Here and there bonfires on the shore marked the sites of new clearings. Once an owl landed on the prow, rested a moment, then glided away. Other boats also dared the darkness. Bobbing lanterns and splashing oars and the cries of lookouts filled the river all the way to Cincinnati, where they arrived at midnight.

The fog over the wharves was luminous with torches. Every manner of craft jostled for space on the riverfront, keelboats and canoes, pirogues, dugouts, sneakboxes, rafts. Despite the hour, men were loading and unloading, driving herds of pigs onto the docks, carrying sacks on their shoulders.

It seemed unnatural to Ely, all this bustle in the middle of the night. In the face of so many people, he felt as helpless about picking up the giant's trail as Owen had felt in the woods. "Oh, Lord," he said, "what do we do now?"

"If you'll stay with the horses, I'll go round the inns and make inquiries," said Owen, who felt cheered by the city bustle. "Our great brute couldn't have passed through here unremarked."

"I'll sit tight," Ely said gratefully.

Owen slipped into the fog like a seed dropped into cotton. Ely squatted against a barrel to wait, while the horses, fidgety from their days on the boat, pawed and stamped the boards of the dock. He watched the river slide past, but could not shut his ears to the city. Shouts, hammers, scrape of crates, rumble of wheels. Too many blamed people, he thought. Even an eight-foot-tall bearman might get lost in these crowds. He recalled every clue he had picked up about the giant —from the terrified woman in Roma, from the spice girl, innkeepers, farmers, teamsters, children, from the old man in the ruined village, from everyone who had glimpsed the big fellow—and still he could not tell what sort of creature he was chasing. Was it a beast? A savage? An idiot who didn't know his own strength? An overgrown child, mute and homeless? While Ely sat wondering, all around him boatmen called to one another in the fog.

An hour passed, and still no sign of the lawyer. Maybe he found a lady to sweet-talk, Ely figured. A place the size of Cincinnati might supply a dozen out-landish beauties to rival Mrs. Forbes. Thinking of the Englishwoman, he was reminded of once having seen, on somebody's mantel, a jar full of dried flowers. A breath would have shattered them. The pale face of Mrs. Forbes, like a field of new-fallen snow, dissolved away in his drowsiness and in its place rose the high Indian cheekbones and dark braids of Rain Hawk, and the unsettling green stare.

Shortly before sunrise two draft horses muscled through the fog onto Ely's dock, hauling a wagon loaded with barrels. The iron-rimmed wheels and iron-shod hooves clacked over the planks; the barrels thunked together hollowly. The driver was a girl, propped on the seat with legs tucked under a patchwork skirt and eyes closed.

The horses kept straight on toward Ely, shoulders bunching at each step. When they smelled the river they stopped, and the girl opened her eyes suddenly, the way a doll will do when it's tipped. "You Captain Jukes?" she asked, blinking.

"I sure ain't," said Ely. "What you needing him for?"

"He's the one sells us the gunpowder."

Her face looked as featureless as goose down. Nine years old? Ten? About the age his sister Caroline had been when she died. He glanced at the load of empty barrels. "Gunpowder?"

"Usually my daddy comes, but he's shot in the ham."

Ely drew close to her, leaned his elbows on the ironbound wheel. "What does your daddy do with all that gunpowder?"

"Sells it to the Indians."

"What Indians?"

"The ones up north around Tippecanoe."

"Mercy, child, don't you know those are *English* Indians?"

The girl teetered sleepily, then caught her balance with a start. "All I know is my daddy's too shot up to sit in a wagon and he says for me to come get the gunpowder."

"But you can't go selling powder to our enemies."

She studied him through eyes now fully awake, eyes too old for the body that shivered on the seat. "Say, are you law?"

"What's that matter?"

"I ain't got no use for law people." Untucking her legs from the patchwork skirt, she dangled them over the edge of the seat, letting her feet clunk against a brace. She wore a man's boots, with the laces wrapped about her ankles to keep them on. She drew the reins up taut. "I got to find Captain Jukes."

Something in the girl's blank pudding of a face appealed to Ely. Perhaps it was only the memory of Caroline. Wanting to keep her, to protect her from the fog and gunpowder and noisy town, he said, "I like the look of your horses."

"And me," she said. Ely turned away from her in confusion. Could she read his face so easily in the dark? But then she added, "And me, too, I like the looks of them. Good pulling horses." She tucked her feet under the skirt again, slackened the reins, set the handbrake. "Might just as well stay here as anywhere to wait for Captain Jukes to show up."

She crossed her arms and hugged them against her flat chest. It was this unripeness in her that put the ache in Ely's heart—the flat chest waiting for breasts, the snub nose, the unmarked face. He asked, "Where's this Captain Jukes live at?"

"I don't have a notion. All I know is he's supposed to been here by now and loaded me up with gunpowder."

Ely peered into the fog. Where in blazes was the lawyer? He didn't know diddle about most things, but maybe he'd know what to do about gunpowder smuggling. Ely gazed back at the girl with a mixed feeling of outrage and protectiveness. "Why don't you drive on home now, honey, and I'll explain to Captain Jukes."

"I ain't your honey." She hunched forward on the seat. "My daddy sent me after gunpowder, and I got to get it."

"But the Indians he sells it to are killing Americans."

"Who're Americans?" she said, her voice rising quizzically.

Good Lord, he thought, she comes from deeper in the woods than I do. "Why, *everybody* in these parts is American—you and me, my partner out there bumbling around in the fog, this whole city. Even your horses are American horses."

She gazed at him, then at the muscular rumps of the draft horses. After considering for a minute, she loosed the reins from the brake. "He'll beat me purple, if he ain't already dead from that shot."

"Why don't you stay with somebody in town?"

"I don't know a soul in Cincinnati."

Come with me, Ely wanted to say. Be my sister. I'll never beat you, never send you after gunpowder in the middle of the night, never abandon you. But he clenched his teeth and said nothing, ashamed of this foolish longing.

"He'll likely die without me there to fetch for him," she added, "him shot in the ham the way he is." With a kissing sound she called to the horses and swung them away from the river.

Ely watched her, a slight figure swaying on the wagon, until she vanished in the luminous fog. Honey, he thought, as the grate of the wheels dwindled until it was quieter than the lapping river. Honey honey honey.

He lay down with the gun tucked next to his ribs.

[83]

Rats scrabbled inside a tub nearby, oxen grunted, stevedores bellowed songs. Cincinnati was waking up—those parts of it that had ever gone to sleep. But Ely soon blocked out these noises, listening only to the river. Purling water sounds, a mutter of birds, boats jostling at anchor, and underneath it all the surge of the Ohio, big and everlasting, a purr that wore through stone.

Sun buttered the river when Ely awoke. Two pairs of boots squeaked toward him, one of them sounding like crickets, and therefore unmistakably the lawyer's.

Owen came up leading a sallow-faced man by the elbow. "Ely, I'd like you to meet Captain Jukes, who has agreed to show us where he put the fugitive ashore yesterday noon."

Ely stood up and leaned on his rifle, blinking first at his partner, whose breath was tangy with drink, then at this river rat. Jukes had on a red flannel shirt, butternut pants, cowhide boots, and a straw hat as broad as an awning. The face beneath was the color of a lizard's sunless belly. The eyes were too shifty for looking into.

"You deal in gunpowder, Captain Jukes?"

"I deal in about anything you can name," said the man.

"Who buys what you got to sell?"

"Whoever's got the money."

"For only six dollars," Owen repeated soothingly, "the captain will carry us to the spot where the giant swam ashore."

Ely thought about the girl riding home to her ham-shot father, about the soldiers up north who would die because of this man's smuggling. Rifle ball in the gut. Fire in the flesh. But he couldn't solve every crime between here and Roma. There was still the giant to catch. At last he said, "Six dollars?"

"Plus you got to stoke wood, like the big guy done for me."

Ely turned on his partner. "What's he talking about —*wood*? Has he got a boat, or has he got a furnace?"

Owen had expected trouble over this detail, knowing his partner would be suspicious of any new-fangled machine. "In a manner of speaking, he has both."

"Steamboat," Jukes declared.

"What in blazes is a steamboat?"

"A magnificent invention," Owen replied. "It burns wood to heat water for steam, which drives a piston, which turns a wheel, which propels the boat. All quite safe."

"Ride on water with a boiler and have it blow up?" said Ely. "No, thanks. I'll go horseback. You go however you want."

Jukes said, "Unless you cut a road, you can't get there."

"There's other boats, plain old muscle boats."

"But Ely, be reasonable. The captain is ready to depart, and he's the only one who can show us the exact location."

Ely scratched his blaze of hair. He wouldn't feel easy riding with Jukes in a wagon on dry land. And here the lawyer wanted to risk their skins with him and a furnace afloat on the Ohio. It was another piece of foolhardiness, but from a distance it might look like courage. Grudgingly, he said, "All right."

Once on the boat, their horses dancing skittishly on the deck, the deputies watched the crew stowing crates, stacking wood, coiling ropes. Ely snooped around, examining the cargo. Afraid of what he might find, Owen tagged along. Beneath a tarp near one paddle wheel they discovered rifles, blocks of lead, shirts, blankets, barrels reeking of black powder. "By God," Ely swore, "there's enough here to outfit the whole British army."

"But surely it's for our side," Owen protested.

"It's headed the wrong direction to be for our boys. God all-blessed-mighty!" Ely took off his hat, mashed it into a ball, shoved it back on. "Smuggling, murdering, stealing. The whole country's gone rotten with people."

Owen was inclined to agree. But he felt the need to coax his young partner through this leg of the journey. "Granted, Captain Jukes is not the most savory character—"

"If I didn't figure this boat was going to blow up, I'd sink it myself," Ely fumed.

From up in the pilot house the captain was bawling orders through a tin horn. The straw hat shaded his face from the early sun. That's how he keeps it looking like a lizard's belly, thought Ely, who yelled up at him, "When are we leaving?"

"Soon as the sheep get here!" Jukes blared through his horn.

"Sheep?"

"To replace the ones as got scalded last time!"

Scalded? The deputies scrutinized the deck, listening for the boilers. Jukes resumed his bawling of orders; the crewmen scrambled up ladders and down hatches. Ely and Owen exchanged a look of alarm, then went to fetch their horses. Just as they reached the gangway, however, up tramped a herd of sheep, nervous and silent, as if not only their backs but also their tongues were covered in wool. Crowding onto the deck, the sheep formed an impenetrable barrier. While the deputies watched in dismay, the hawsers were cast free and the boat nosed into the river.

"You got us in a fix this time, Mr. Lightfoot."

"We haven't far to go," Owen reassured him. "Only three hours, from what the captain said."

"He swore he saw the giant climb ashore?"

"Yes, and described the location in detail. There's a cliff on the Indiana side, rising straight up from the river, with vines hanging over the top like the forelock on a horse. The face of the cliff is decorated with Indian paintings, and about thirty feet up is a square-mouthed cave."

"Door-in-Rock," Ely said. He had passed it while hunting for Ezra, but the unnatural shape of the cave mouth and the dark stories people told about the place had kept him from stopping to explore.

"You make it sound rather unpleasant," said Owen.

"I just heard about it, is all. People say it's one of the old burying holes."

The boiler grumbled in the bowels of the boat. The

paddle wheels began to churn, sopping the two of them with water. Huddled against the rail, the sheep soon withered to half their former size as the spray matted their wool.

"Shouldn't we go below to stoke?" Owen suggested. "We did promise."

Ely shrugged. "I guess I'd rather look at a furnace than stand here watching those idiot sheep."

Down below they found the boilers already fired to fever pitch, and still the naked stokers were throwing wood into the flames. Rivets stood out black against the glowing iron plates. After one glimpse, the deputies backed away, promise or no promise, and climbed onto the deck to camp between the kegs of gunpowder and the long-suffering herd of sheep.

Ely muttered, "If we ever catch that blame giant, maybe he'll eat you."

"One more hour," was all Owen answered.

The deputies sat leaning against crates, watching the river, listening for any catch in the paddle wheel gears, any screech from the furnace. First Ohio and then Indiana slid by on the right, Kentucky on the left. Brooding on the war, the girl, the eternal sowing and reaping of death in this land, Ely worked himself into such a rage that presently he leaped up and began heaving bags of shot and bundles of rifles over the side.

"What in God's name are you doing?" demanded Owen.

"Give me a hand," Ely grunted, rolling a barrel of gunpowder with his foot.

His partner's anger was so compelling that Owen found himself actually helping lift the barrel over the rail. When Ely came staggering under the weight of more rifles, Owen said, "Have you taken leave of your senses? Can't you be patient for another little while? We must be very close to the place."

Cloaked by spray from the paddle wheel, their labors would be scarcely visible from the pilot house. Nevertheless, Owen glanced around nervously to see whether they had been detected. When he looked back, Ely was hoisting the first sheep overboard.

"No!" Owen begged. "Not livestock, Ely. That's larceny."

Ely flung the sheep into the water, then a second, and was swinging a third one overboard when Jukes roared from the pilot house: "We lost a sheep! Goddammit all to hell, we lost a sheep!"

Hidden by spray, Ely kept right on heaving armfuls of guns and sacks of lead over the rail. Owen hung back, appalled.

Jukes came scrambling down the ladder. "Turn about!" he cried, as he watched the animals dip and wallow astern. "I got to have those sheep!"

"Now you've done it," hissed Owen.

Amid the screaming of gears as the wheels reversed, Ely said, "Get your horse ready. We may have to swim for it."

Wondering what would go first—gears, boiler, paddle wheels, or gunpowder?—Ely did not think of the guard rail. But the sheep suddenly panicked and burst the railing, and the entire herd cascaded into the water. They clung together in a woollen knot and swam for shore. This sight so frenzied the pilot that the steamboat was soon lodged sideways in the river, bow and stern mired in sandbars and the sidewheels uselessly churning.

Ely hooted with delight. While Jukes led his crew to the stern, bellowing after his lost sheep, the deputies flung a gangway from the bow and guided their horses down onto the sandbar and splashed through shallows onto the Indiana shore.

Owen peered hopefully downstream, then lit with a smile. "There it is, unless I'm badly mistaken."

And sure enough, there at the next bend was a creamy cliff, with a square opening halfway up, stringy forelock of vines on the top, paintings of birds and people and fish on the rockface.

"That's Door-in-Rock, all right," said Ely uneasily.

"According to our Captain Jukes, this is where the giant leaped overboard yesterday."

They looked back at the steamboat caught galley-wonkers in the river. Jukes shouted orders through his tin horn, the straw hat flapping on his head like a pale bird. The sheep had reached the far shore and were munching their way into Kentucky.

By dint of shifting cargo and swearing in three languages, the crew eventually got the craft afloat. As Ely watched the boat puff its way around the bend, the image of the cavemouth hung before him, unnaturally square, black, a doorway into stone. Thoughts of the bearman holed up inside that cave dragged his head back around and quenched his smile.

Noticing his somber mood, Owen said, "Do you suppose he's in there?"

"There's only two ways to find out. We camp down here and wait to see if he comes after food. Or we go in and look."

Suspecting that his headstrong partner would choose the blunt approach, Owen said, "What harm is there in waiting?"

"If I've got to run into him, I'd just as soon do it before he gets good and hungry."

Owen had to admit there was wisdom in that.

8

THE DEPUTIES MADE CAMP ON THE SHORE IN A
tangle of swamp oak and willow and blackberries.
The cliff rose above them, shaggy with ferns, and
higher up it was patchy with moss and lichens, and
still higher it was bare gray stone. The crown thrust
at the sky like the snout of a whale leaping above the
sea of vegetation. The deputies avoided speaking of
the giant, but thought about nothing else, circling round
and round the single worry like two dogs chained to
a post.

Ely planned to wait for morning before trying the
cave. He cleaned his rifle, checked the flint, sharpened
his knife against his leggins, all the while keeping an
eye on the square opening in the cliff. Next he gathered ferns and willow branches for beds. As he worked
along the shore, muskrats and frogs splashed into the
water ahead of him. A long-legged crane, blinking its
great orange eyes at him, browsed for seed in the
tangle of burnt-out wildflowers near the river's edge.
Bending over the shallows, Ely saw, beneath the reflections of clouds, the sleek shapes of fish. Every now

and again he would peer up at the cliff, but nothing moved in the cavemouth.

After finishing his own bed he made one for Owen, spreading willow branches, and on top of them a heap of ferns. He caught himself whistling, cut off the sound abruptly, then shrugged and took up the tune again. No point in keeping quiet. Unless the giant was deaf or far away, he would have heard the racket of the steamboat and the shouting crewmen and the nickering horses.

Meanwhile, Owen filled his tin cup with blackberries, ate the juicy lumps one by one, then picked the cup full again. The fruits hung in clusters from arching vines, each one as black and multiple as the eye of an ant. "What a magnificent fruit," he declared. "Although I could do without the stickers."

"No sweets without thorns," said Ely. One of Pappy's many sayings. Old saws for every occasion. Worn phrases littered Ely's mind like water-smoothed pebbles on the bed of a creek.

When Owen had enough of berry-picking, he found Ely sitting on one of the newly made beds, stitching a torn moccasin. Owen sagged onto his own mattress of ferns and gave a contented sigh.

"How's that feel?" said Ely.

"Delightful. You do have a knack for this sort of thing."

"I get by."

Owen stretched out. "I believe you could be set down in the middle of a perfect wilderness, and still prosper."

"The one we're in ain't perfect by a long shot."

"What would you change to make it so?"

"I'd get rid of the people." Drawing a thong tight in the moccasin, Ely thought about the girl in the patchwork skirt and her daddy who smuggled gunpowder. He gave a grunt of disgust. "Starting with that Jukes. There's nothing lower than a man who makes his living off people killing each other."

"He is rather a vile sort, I agree." Owen lay on the ferns, hands laced beneath his head. This frontier warfare seemed to him a deeper mystery than birth or love or the sprouting of seeds. Armed gangs butchering one another. Perhaps the spirit of the wilderness had entered men's souls and corrupted their reason. Gibbon had described it well, this tide of barbarism. "How do you suppose things will turn out?" he asked.

"The war? Depends how Perry does with his ships on Lake Erie. If he loses, we'd all best move back across the Ohio."

Owen shifted on his bed from one aching haunch to the other. The broken ferns smelled of burnt coffee, an odor that aroused in him thoughts of supper. He rose stiffly. "Perhaps I should gather some kindling."

Ely made no offer to help. Instead he sat watching uprooted trees slide by on the river. The same current was shoving settlers into the heart of the country, as if the river itself were determined to fill the woods with axes and guns. A flatboat drifted by, dragging an uproar of children squealing and cows mooing. "Halloo the shore! Where you two headed?" a man cried. Ely kept his eyes on the river without answering. He tried to squeeze the war and the giant out of his mind, tried to forget settlers and cities. His heart slowed to the pace of the current. Miracles of birds wheeled above him, fish gleamed in the water at his feet, grass spoke to him in a thousand tongues.

After a spell his solitude was broken by the lawyer's voice. "Would you mind building a fire?" Owen dumped an armload of wood clattering on the ground.

Ely scowled at him, and the valley was peopled again, for the lawyer with his boiled shirt and shaved face and gold-rimmed glasses was a walking reminder of towns. Banks seemed to hide in his pockets, libraries spoke through his lips, fences stiffened his collar, brick houses slept in his eyes, paving stones clung to his feet. Ely said, "You ain't hot enough without a fire?"

"I thought it would be pleasant to have some coffee."

"We're maybe caught up with the giant, and you're wanting coffee?" Ely said. Nearly three weeks of riding and sleeping with the fat, high-talking, tenderfooted lawyer had not made him seem any more probable. But what if he's the common sort in the cities, Ely wondered, and I'm the odd one?

While Owen heated water, Ely went to inspect the cliff. The last thing in the world he wanted to do was climb up into that cave looking for a giant. Why did I have to find that blasted dwarf dead in the spice girl's stump? And Rain Hawk! Chanting songs in her mother's tongue. Screeching at me about rabbits and bearmen. She's enough to cure a guy of females for life.

Rain had washed out any tracks the giant might

have left in the mud at the base of the cliff. A white-ringed viper uncurled from the path in front of Ely and stabbed into the river. Viewed up close, what he had taken to be paintings on the rock turned out to be carvings of birds and other beasts, with stain rubbed in the furrows. Directly below the cavemouth he found a notch chiseled into the stone at the height of his waist. An arm's length above it was another. Steps, he thought. Peering up the cliff he saw a row of them, each one shaped like a half-moon with the flat side down, each step as wide as the spread fingers of a hand. Judging from the distance between foot holes, whoever had carved them was long-legged. There was nothing but the weight of dread to keep him from climbing right up to the cave. No, no, he thought. Wait for morning. Fresh muscles. New light.

In camp, listening to Ely's description while pouring coffee, Owen asked, "Who do you suppose fashioned those steps?"

"Same as did the carvings," said Ely. "The Old People."

"The Mound Builders?"

"Whatever you call them. The old ones." Tribes more ancient than the Indians, a vanished race who had buried their dead in raised mounds of clay, had built forts on bluffs above the Scioto and Miami, had carved figures into cliffs near the mouth of the Muskingum, had raised earthworks in the gigantic shapes of birds and snakes and dragons like vast scrawlings in a language meant to be read from the moon.

Owen said, "Do you really mean to go up there looking for him in the morning?"

"I said I'd go up, didn't I? You think I won't?" Ely snatched a fistful of mint and crushed it, holding it to his nose. "I don't figure you'd risk *your* neck going up there."

Nettled, Owen demanded, "Haven't I come this far? And didn't you think I'd quit on that first day out from Roma?"

"You surprised me by sticking it out. I'll give you that much. But has it ever crossed your mind to climb up that cliff?"

Owen gazed at the wall of limestone, shadowed now, the sun gone down behind. Midway up, a rectangle of annihilating blackness. "No, I can't say that it has."

"There you are." Ely spat into the fire, his body tense. By and by he took out the flute and began playing. The sound was like honey on his nerves.

Owen drew his telescope from the instrument case and peered at the cave, but could not penetrate the blackness. Nothing would suffice but naked eyes. Why not mine? Would Lewis and Clark have sat here on their buttocks, paralyzed? Quickly, before his resolve could fade, he put away the telescope and set off along the shore.

Lowering the flute, Ely called after him, "Where are you going?" When the lawyer kept right on crashing through the willows, Ely shouted, "Mr. Lightfoot, you ain't even got a gun! It's too dark to see where you're going! You'll fall in the river! Mr. Lightfoot!"

Owen crept out of sight beyond a shoulder of rock. He'll be back directly, Ely thought. For a while he blew tunes on the flute. But worry eventually dried up

the music in his throat, and he sat listening for footsteps. Night thickened.

By the time Owen stumbled into the firelight again
it was so black out that Ely figured he must have been
asking directions from owls. His suit smelled of mint
and sweat and blackberry.

"You made it back," said Ely, relieved.

"More or less." Owen ran a finger inside his soiled
collar. Only then, watching the hand quiver, did Ely
realize how far the man had pushed himself.

"Here's some coffee left." Ely took the lawyer's
shaking hands and wrapped them around the cup.
Wanting to comfort him, he said, "All right, you
showed me something. I'd never have gone out there
again tonight, not for anything."

Owen slumped near the fire, sipping at the cup,
shivering. His suit was beginning to look as if it had
been tailored for a larger man. In a whisper he said,
"He's up there."

Ely felt a dizzying rush of blood. "You saw him?"

"He was sitting on the ledge in front of the cave
with his legs hanging down. The feet were as big as
anvils. He was making a deep noise in his chest, a
groaning, like an organ."

Both men stopped talking, stopped breathing, and
listened. Catbirds mewed in the willows. Sap crackled
in the fire.

At length Owen broke their stillness by saying, "He
stopped his groaning just as soon as you quit playing
the flute, and he lifted up his feet, and that was the last
I saw of him."

"Then you came on back?"

"No, then I climbed a few steps up that cliff. Three steps, maybe four. But I couldn't go any higher. I wanted to, I truly did, but I just couldn't." Owen's voice was as frayed as a tablecloth that has been washed and folded a thousand times.

"What did you figure on doing if you got up there, without any light or gun?"

"I don't know. I didn't think it through very clearly. I suppose I wanted to prove to myself that I could do it." He took off the spectacles and rubbed knuckles into each eye. Then he stared at Ely in a frenzy of exhaustion. "But I couldn't, I just couldn't. It was as if the whole cliff weighed down on me."

"You showed me something, Mr. Lightfoot," Ely said again, resting a hand on his shoulder, "you truly did. Now you sleep, and I'll keep watch."

For another moment, Owen stared at him with those wild, exhausted eyes, shrunken, humbled, all the high talk wrung out of him, and then he slumped onto his mattress of ferns. Soon he was twitching with sleep. He whimpered but did not stir when Ely covered him with a blanket.

Ely sat with his back to the fire, gun in the crook of his arm, watching the moon-yellowed cliff. His eyes smarted, but he kept them open. Sleep stroked his head with a lulling hand, sang to him with the voice of Rain Hawk crooning her Shawnee melodies. Fighting to stay awake, he fixed on the night's sensations: the gleaming muscle of the river, the rasping of bullfrogs and locusts, the must of woodsmoke. But his senses grew numb. Even fear of what might slouch down from the cave could not protect him from the weariness of three weeks on the trail. Sleep rose over his body like floodwater.

Toward morning one of the horses whinnied. Ely opened his eyes with the suddenness of a sprung trap, but held still, arms across his lifted knees, head pillowed on his arms. The gun lay against his thighs. In the gray light he could see the horses, their legs still hobbled. Instead of grazing, they had their muzzles lifted, ears pricked forward. He strained to hear what they were hearing. Beside him, Owen breathed with the steady wheeze of sleep. Embers sizzled in the fire. His own heart pounded in his ears. Otherwise, not a sound, no locusts calling, no morning songs from the birds, no courting from the bullfrogs.

Eyes wide open to see in the faint light, Ely forced himself to keep a sleeper's stillness. Nothing moved except the river. But looming against the river's gleam, right in the middle of the path, was the shadow of a massive stump. Had there been a stump there last night? Surely, surely. His eyes ached from staring at it. He scolded himself for this child's fancy, turning wood into giant's flesh. But when the moon broke through its cloud cover he could see that the stump had a head on top of it, shaggy with hair, as large as a prize pumpkin. Then he knew it was the bearman, hunkered there next to the river, watching him.

Ely stared back. He felt as if the attention of the entire silent woods were fixed on him. He feared his bones would snap from the pressure. The giant squatted there like a boulder, a concentration of darkness. Sweat stung Ely's face, and his fingers grasping the rifle cramped with the desire to shoot. But he fought his body to stillness. All the dawn was reduced to these two watching presences, himself and the bear-man.

The sky behind the giant slowly brightened, outlining him against the river. To Ely he seemed less threatening now, cut off from the night and the woods. Now he was only a huge man crouching there, uprooted by dawn from the strength of earth.

A crane whistled by overhead, and Ely flinched at the noise. The giant straightened up suddenly, huge against the glitter of river, as tall and thick as a bear. Now it comes, thought Ely, his throat squeezed shut as if a great hand were already wrapped around it. Even as he swung the rifle toward the hulking shape, the giant raised his arm. With a rock? A gun? Shoot him now, *shoot shoot shoot*, put a ball through that shaggy head. But he's a man, Ely kept telling himself, only a man, and you can't just kill him like any beast. The giant lowered his arm, cocked his head as if listening, and then turned and stalked back along the river path into the brightening sky. Step by step he climbed the rockface, never looking back at Ely, who never let go of his gun.

9

I N THE DAWN'S THREADBARE LIGHT, ELY DISCOVERED
the enormous bootprints within a yard of the fire.
Casting a huge moonshadow, the giant must have
watched them sleep for some time, because the tracks
nearest the fire were pressed deep into the earth, as if
the great man had squatted there, rocking on heel and
toe.

Ely placed one foot in each of the prints and bent
down over the lawyer. Imagining himself inside the
giant's body, arms as strong as trees, he studied this
sleeper who had come with chains and affidavits in
search of him. Fat city man asleep, mind full of books,
mouth full of words. He would die so easily.

At that moment the lawyer shuddered awake, eyes
goggling up at him in terror. Owen cried out, hunching into a ball, arms thrown over his face. After a
moment he uncurled and scolded, "Ely, what on earth
are you doing?"

Ely stepped out of the giant's footprints, lowered
his hands. "I was play-acting."

"You scared the living daylights out of me. Here I am, dreaming about him, and I wake up to find this dreadful shape towering over me." Owen shivered, fitting the spectacles onto his nose. When he spied the giant's tracks where Ely had been standing, panic wrenched his face again. "Good God!"

"Rest easy," said Ely. "He's been visiting, but he's gone."

"He was right *there*? He could have killed us."

"If he'd meant to kill us, we'd be dead now, squashed like that rabbit the spice girl left on your steps." Saying this, Ely thought he knew why she had left that bloody present. It was a reminder of what the bearman had done to the rabbity dwarf, a warning of what he might do to anybody fool enough to chase him.

"Then why did he come so close?" Owen said.

"How do I know? I ain't a giant. Maybe he was lonely. Maybe he likes fire. Maybe he was just sizing us up, seeing who was camped down here below his cave."

Owen gazed along the trail where he had walked last night. He could not imagine walking there again. It was a physical impossibility, like passing through the eye of a needle.

Ely tugged the hunting shirt off over his head, then the linsey undershirt. As he began loosening the rope belt of his breeches, Owen said, "Now what are you doing?"

"Going to clean myself."

Ely splashed naked into the water, a scrawny, long-limbed boy with skin pale everywhere except the weather-darkened face and hands. From a passing skiff a female voice yelled, "Halloo, bather! Whoee!" Embarrassed, Owen turned back to the fire.

A few minutes later Ely came back dripping, shaking water from his mane of red hair. There was a fierce composure in the way he went about dressing himself, honing the knife on his leggins, examining the tinder in his firekit and the flint in his gun. Last of all he drew from his saddlebags two candle stubs, several pine knots, and the frying pan, and these he stuffed into the pouch in his shirtfront.

Owen watched these preparations in puzzled silence. Ely shone with the clear singleness of a person in a trance. When it seemed he would leave without saying another word, Owen offered, "I'll take my gun and keep watch."

"I'd appreciate that, sir. If he sticks his nose out before I get up there, would you fire in the air?" Ely gave a tug at the rope belt, which was already drawn so tightly that Owen was amazed it did not cut the boy in two. He seemed to have shrunk, until there was nothing left of him but muscle, bone, and will. "If I come back out in one piece, you're all right. But if he comes out by himself, you'd better get on Blackstone and ride."

Owen dried his palms on the mired breast of his shirt, his best courtroom shirt, which he would burn if he ever got home in it alive to Roma. "Ely, we never promised to bring him back or die trying. We could summon help. Suppose he pushes you—"

Ely answered grimly: "Suppose this, suppose that!

How can I say what he'll do? I don't even know for sure what he *is*. I been thinking about him every minute for three weeks, and I'm still in the dark. I'm done with thinking. Now I just got to go fetch him or else I got to pack up and go home. And I don't mean to leave without meeting him. I've got to see him or bust."

As he strode away, the breeches flapping loose on him, Owen called, "If he shows himself I'll shoot him, if you'd like."

Halfway through the mint and brambles to the cliff, Ely swung around. "No, sir. If I'd wanted him shot, I could have done that already this morning. I want him alive."

Owen sat glumly on his mattress of ferns to wait, the rifle across his knees, his mind creeping into the cave and burrowing down through branching midnight tunnels into the earth.

At the spot near the cliff where the giant had hunkered down to watch him earlier that morning, Ely found a gourd heaped with porcupine quills, bear claws, and woodpecker bills. What's he mean, leaving me this? A threat from the killer of bears? Ely stirred the gourd with his finger, thinking, I've killed bears, too, big ones, and worse. Picking out a few of the claws, he wrapped them in a wad of linen and tucked them into his shirt.

He gazed up the cliff at the steps gouged into the rock, gathering himself. Once he put his foot in the first notch, he would have to keep climbing, just as he had been forced to keep on with the hunt from the moment he touched the dwarf. A fellow gets caught up in a current, and there's no quitting until it lets him go.

Then he began to climb, lifting himself from notch to notch, the stone rough against fingers and moccasins. A dozen feet up, as he reached for the next hole, he touched the coiled body of a snake. He jerked his hand away, almost losing his perch. Then, calming, he drew his knife, scraped the hole clean, and twisted around to watch a blacksnake, lank and harmless, tumble to the ground. Blacksnake, warblers singing— he should have known better than to step outdoors on that morning three weeks ago.

He climbed on, hugging the rockface. One step beneath the ledge, he rested. Far below, dwindled to the size of a rag doll, Owen peered up at him through the spyglass. For a moment Ely saw him again through the giant's eyes, and felt an utter scorn for this toy of a man and all his kind who had blundered into this wild country hoping to tame it with law books and clocks and saws.

Suddenly there came a scratching on the ledge above him. Ely stiffened and glanced down, judging the best way to land from thirty feet. Owen calmly waved his arm, a puppet's motion, but what he was trying to signal, Ely could not guess. Presently the scratching ceased. Squirrel? Bird? Or was the giant up there, waiting for him to risk his skull above the ledge?

The only way to find out was to look. He drew his knife, filled his lungs, ready to let out a fierce cry, and heaved himself onto the ledge. It was deserted. He tumbled forward onto hands and knees, panting, the cry lodged in his throat.

Before him the cave gaped like the square opening of a mine. Cold air seeped out, bearing the stench of the giant and a whiff of woodsmoke. There were designs scratched into the stone around the entrance, like picture writing. Marks of the Old People? No telling what they meant. Sunlight angled into the opening, and there, on the border between light and shadow, Ely found a seashell filled with blackberries. Seashell? Seven hundred miles from the ocean? He knelt down and sniffed the berries, turning them over in their shell as if they were pearls, and then he tipped them into his mouth. Sweet, juice the color of night.

Beyond the reach of sunlight the cave receded into darkness blacker than the spaces between stars. Ely gazed into it with terror, the same terror that seized him from time to time in his bed when the certainty of death shook him in its cold fist. The giant-laden breath of the cave chilled him as it dried his sweat. Death's certain, by and by. But not today, he swore, not, by God, today. Quit your thinking and go in there after him.

His hands shook so that it took him several licks at the flint before he had a spark in the tinder. He puffed it into flame, lit one of the candles, and with the candle lit a resiny pine knot. Carried before him in the skillet, the knot cast a flickering orange glow onto the walls of the cave. Litter of fallen rock beneath his feet, black passages opening to left and right, downhanging teeth of stone overhead. As he stole forward, shadows closed behind him like water behind a boat. With every step into the guts of the hill, his breath came shallower. Each pace added to the weight of fear he carried, until he felt as heavy as the giant, and yet he kept on, pace after pace, with the whole cliff riding on his shoulders.

Black everywhere beyond the guttering glow of his torch. Sounds of water dripping, rats or mice scurrying. The passage narrowed, ceiling lowered, stone teeth nearly raking his scalp. Ely bent over and crept on, rifle in one hand, skillet with its flaming knot in the other. How the giant must shrink himself to squeeze through here. Then suddenly the tunnel bellied out into a cavern wider and higher than his light could fill. Here the bearman's stench was more potent even than the smell of burning pitch. Dry leaves underfoot. Crack of twigs. Bones?

Ely froze, breath held—and still heard breathing, not his own, ponderous, slow, as if it were the wheezing of the hill itself. Where is he? Where? Eyes smarting from the torch, he stared and stared until he made out, at some unmeasurable distance across the gulf of blackness, the red embers of a fire. Lying beside it, a sleeper's body like a fallen tree.

The vast breathing filled the cavern. Ely wanted to howl. He feared the pressure of the giant's nearness would shove him out through the tunnel, down the cliff, onto his horse, and all the way back to Roma, empty-handed, white-faced, screaming. Gulping the foul air, he turned halfway around. The going out would be easier than the coming in. But down below the lawyer would be waiting, glad to see him fail. And besides, thought Ely, I'm too close to this wonder for turning back.

He steadied himself. Quietly, he set down the pan with its guttering flame, to free both hands for the gun, then pointed the barrel at the sleeping giant. He wet his lips, and in a cracking voice declared: "Get up slow. Slow, now, you hear me? And raise your arms up over your head."

The massive breathing caught like a saw hitting a knot, then resumed faster, lighter, and down near the fire two yellow eyes snapped open, reflecting the torchlight back at him. The eyes lifted from the floor, rising and rising toward the vault of the cavern, higher than any man's eyes should rise, and beneath them a body surged to its feet so cumbrously that for a moment Ely thought it might really be a bear rearing on its hind legs.

"Hold still right there!" Ely shouted, his words rumbling in the belly of stone.

The eyes blinked impassively, glittering eyes as big as soup spoons. The bearman lumbered into the torchlight, his splayed feet in their boots scuffing over the stone like feed sacks dragged on a floor.

"I said hold still!" But the scuffing drew closer. "Stop, or by God I'll shoot!" Ely bellowed. Yet he knew, even before the echoes had died away, that talk was useless on this one.

Scrape, scrape, heavy boots on stone, shaggy head lurching nearer. Ely edged away from the torch, gun lifted, hammer drawn. The giant stooped down and seized the frying pan by the handle. He'll fling the fire into the tunnel, thought Ely, scrambling backward. It's either kill him right now, or be trapped in this hole with him in the devil's own darkness. He squinted along the barrel, cheek against the gun's cold stock. Pull the trigger and be done with it. He imagined the roar the gun would make in the cavern, the ball ripping through the great head. But instead of flinging the torch away, the giant held it up to his face, turning it this way and that, like a child presented with a wondrous toy. He gazed at it the way Ely had gazed at the giant's own bootprint in the mud, and that wondering look kept Ely from shooting. He lifted his cheek from the gun and studied the torchlit giant. Black beard, silvery on the tips, growing almost up to the yellow eyes. Daub of red paint, still wet, on his forehead. Stiff black hair matted with dirt and bits of leaves like a winter bush. Everything oversize, the Adam's apple bulging under the beard, the shoulders in their greasy coat, the fingers like tree roots holding the skillet. A necklace of teeth curved across his chest, and pinned below it was an ink-stained scrap of leather.

Lit by the torch, the bearman made a luminous target. But Ely knew already that he could not just shoot him, not so long as there was a way of escaping his long arms. "Come on peaceful, come on outside with me," he said, again feeling the uselessness of talk as soon as the words had left his tongue.

For answer, the giant held out his free hand, the palm dirt-caked, and in it was a necklace of bear teeth strung on a thong.

"No," Ely said, shaking his head. Gift or threat,

whatever it was, he had no desire for it. He could read nothing in the yellow gleaming eyes, certainly no fear of death.

The bearman never glanced at the rifle, only stared down into Ely's face. Arm thrust out, necklace dangling from one great fist, he took a step forward. Ely backed along the wall, still shaking his head, no no no, feeling his way, groping for the tunnel. The way out, the way out. The giant lurched after him, pace for pace, the torch flaring in one hand and the beartooth necklace shimmering in the other.

Suddenly Ely's fingers groped into air, and he turned, thinking he had reached the tunnel. But it was only a pocket in the wall, and round it swelled the huge shadow closing on him. He whirled, found the giant looming over him with arms spread. He darted to the side, but the giant caught up with him in two strides, trapped him against the rock, and when Ely lifted the gun the giant snatched it from his hands and flung it clattering away. Ely crouched there, gasping, eyes squeezed shut, praying, O Lord, let it be quick, remembering the rabbit, the dwarf.

His heart kept thudding, and still no blow fell. What's he waiting for? What? Opening his eyes warily, Ely discovered the giant hunched motionless above him and gazing calmly down, hand thrust forward with the necklace. The big man gave a grunt, a sound as deep and lordly as the bellow of a bull.

Amazed to be alive, Ely nodded, leaning forward, and the giant settled the necklace over his head. Teeth showed grinning through the black beard. The giant

let out another bullish grunt and began signing rap-
idly with his fingers. He ended by touching one hand
to Ely's necklace and the other hand to the necklace
at his own throat. Again Ely nodded, overawed, realizing now why he and Owen had not been killed
the night before while they slept at the fire, why he
had not been brushed like a fly from the cliff, why he
had not been crushed against the cavern wall.

"Brothers," Ely said. He fingered the necklace, laid
a hand on his heart, squeezed his palms together in
sign of brotherhood, exaggerating each gesture as he
would for a simpleton.

The giant wrapped Ely in those tree-limb arms and
lifted him into the air, but carefully, as if hugging a
baby. Their foreheads pressed together, and Ely felt
on his brow the cool smear of paint. After setting him
down again, the giant stood there with empty mud-
caked palm held out, waiting.

Grasping now what these gifts meant—the bear
claws and berries and necklace—Ely fumbled in his
pouch until he found the two candle stubs, the only
presents he had, and these he laid in the big man's
hand. The giant rolled them in his cupped palm, lit
them from the torch, dripped tallow into the skillet
and stuck them there beside the flaming pine knot. Then
he shuffled away across the cavern bearing this dish of
fire. He peered back once over his shoulder to make
sure Ely was following.

Ely gaped in wonder at what the light revealed.
The walls of the chamber were honeycombed with
nooks the same half-moon shape as the steps in the

cliff, only much larger, large enough to hold the skeletons of men. Curved ribs gleamed at him like the tusks of boars. Crowded around the bones were clay pots, ornaments of copper and pearl, pipes carved with the figures of birds and snakes, flint spearheads, necklaces of blue beads and carved mica, pearly seashells. In some of the tombs there were freshly gathered berries and nuts and bundles of roots—the giant's gifts for the dead in the underworld?

The big man slouched from grave to grave, scooping these treasures in his great hands and holding them near the light for Ely to admire. The huge head cocked to one side and grinned. Ely put away his fear, feeling himself in the presence of a gigantic child, and then he, too, handled these ornaments of the dead with awe, fingering the ice-smooth carvings, hefting ax-heads, wondering where these people had found copper and mica, wondering what hands had carried these shells all the way from the sea.

The giant led him the circuit of the cavern, stopping at each grave. Along the way, Ely retrieved his gun and slung it over his shoulder. When they arrived at the passage that led outside, the bearman lifted his arms, the curve of bear teeth glinting at his throat, and gestured at the nest of tombs. He thumped his chest and roared exultantly.

"Yes," Ely replied, signing with hand gestures, "these are your people. Your people sleep here."

The giant bent over him and rested a meaty hand on his shoulder. He left it there a few seconds, long enough for Ely again to feel breakable under the tree strength of this man. Yet the touch was delicate, as if the giant were handling a bird.

The great yellow cat's eyes blinked down at Ely. No thoughts to read there, only distance, strangeness.

The hand lifted, and the giant rocked on his heels. Now we must go into the daylight, Ely signed to him. We must go on a trip, a long way, half a moon. Unsure of his power over the big man, Ely turned his back on the cavern, on the honeycombed dead, and motioned for the giant to follow him into the tunnel. And sure enough, the feedsack steps scuffed behind him down the passage and all the way to the square mouth of the cave.

In the painful daylight Ely snuffed the candles and put them in the giant's waiting palm. Gift of brotherhood. Two sticks of fire. The burning pine knot he threw into the river, and stuffed the skillet into his shirt. In the daylight he could see that words had been inked onto the patch of leather on the big man's chest, but he would have to leave the reading of them to Owen.

Beside him on the ledge, the giant hesitated, looking down at the camp where Owen still kept his vigil. The Ohio glinted like liquid pewter. Ely waved to the lawyer, jerking his thumb at the slung rifle, touching his forehead and then pointing at the big man. But Owen gave no sign of having understood. He jumped up and flourished his gun, as if to signify that he could be relied upon.

Ely descended first, not wanting Owen to shoot the giant in panic. The big man climbed after, easing down the cliff with ponderous grace.

"You can put up that gun!" Ely shouted as the two of them approached the camp.

Owen had climbed onto his horse, but kept the rifle at the ready. He watched them come with his face screwed tight. "Is he quite safe?"

"I'm back here alive, ain't I?" said Ely.

Owen looked from the brute to Ely and back to the awesome brute. "How did you manage it?"

"Never mind how. He's here. Now kindly put that gun away and climb down and get hold of yourself before you spook him."

Owen clung to the saddle. Blackstone sensed his fear and danced about. "Mightn't he have some weapon in his shirt? A knife perhaps?"

"Can't you see he don't *need* weapons?"

Owen ran his gaze nervously over the prisoner, the body in its leather garments as thick as a courthouse pillar, wide, blank face like that of an ox, eyes the color of butter. "Yes, yes, I see what you mean. Yet he followed you like a pet bear."

"The only thing that matters is he's here," said Ely, "and now we got to go back. I think he'll come. I *hope* he'll come."

"I never imagined I'd see you alive, let alone parading him out—" Owen stopped abruptly, realizing they had been speaking in front of the giant as though he were as ignorant of speech as an ox. He glanced at the bearded face. No sign of intelligence in those eyes. "Does he understand what we're saying?"

"I don't believe so. But I can't be sure."

"Did you tell him he's under arrest on charges of murder?"

[115]

"I didn't tell him a thing."

Then Owen noticed the twin necklaces, bits of gleaming bone at each man's throat, and on both of their foreheads a slash of red. Blood? No—paint. He looked more sharply at that colossal figure who towered behind Ely. "Why, Ely, you're a genius." Owen laughed in admiration. "You've found out the peddler's secret, the power he exercised over this Pennsylvania ironman."

"Leave it be, Mr. Lightfoot," Ely answered.

"You did, you most certainly did. Just look at him, fawning after you. He takes you for his new master, his keeper, his protector."

"Please, Mr. Lightfoot, don't go on about it." Ashamed, Ely kicked dirt on the fire and went to yank at the cinch on Babe's saddle. The big man slouched along at his heels.

10

EVEN WITH THE GIANT HIDDEN IN THE BRUSH AND
Owen in his store-bought suit and velvet tie yelling offers of money from the shore, no boat would
stop for them. Folks knew better. The river was full
of stories about travelers who had been lured ashore
and waylaid by Indians and thieves. The only way
back to Cincinnati was overland. The giant broke a
trail through reeds, snapped off low-slung limbs, waded
through brier patches with brambles dragging behind
him like the traces of a runaway horse. Sometimes
riding, sometimes afoot, the deputies followed grimly,
licking blood that seeped from scratches on their faces,
gasping for breath as if the air were thick with feathers.

They reached the city late in the afternoon. Heaped
wagons trundled by, wheeling into muddy side streets
where hammers banged and saws flashed and houses
rose like mushrooms. Hogs rooted through slops on
the wooden sidewalks or lay in the gutters damming
sewage with their fat haunches. Gangs of soldiers,
pausing on their way north to the war, loitered and

bragged in the shade of stores, rifles slung from shoulders and pistols shoved in belts. Street vendors hawked ginseng, clocks, tea, potatoes.

Everyone kept a healthy distance from this odd trio—the lawyer in his bedraggled suit, the boy in deerskin with flaming hair and excitable eyes, and the huge creature who shambled menacingly behind them. People slipped into doorways, climbed onto horses, clearing a broad path. Shutters clapped to, eyes peered around the corners of buildings, children pointed.

"I can't say that I blame them," said Owen, who had not relaxed for a moment since Ely descended from the cave with the prisoner in tow. To all appearances this ironman was a stupid brute, as witless as a draft horse. The leather tag pinned to his chest, inscribed by various hands, seemed to bear witness to his docility: GUIDE THIS FELLOW TO MARIETTA. HE'S PEACE-ABLE. HE UNDERSTANDS SIGN. TAKE HIM ON TO CINCINNATI. HE'S WORTH MORE THAN HIS PASSAGE IN WORK. FEED HIM UP. And finally: DELIVER HIM TO DOOR-IN-ROCK. And so the big man had been passed along from hand to hand, like a package.

But if indeed he had mashed the dwarf into that stump, Owen reflected, and if he were guilty of even a tenth part of all those feats that had been blamed on him, then he was a thoroughly dangerous customer, no matter how peaceful he might appear. And what if he were merely an outrider for hordes of barbarians living out west beyond the Mississippi, savages more formidable even than the Huns and Goths who had conquered Rome?

"No tavern's going to put us up," said Ely.

"There's no harm in trying," Owen said. "And keep your eye out for a barbershop. What I crave more than anything is a shave and a haircut. I've almost forgotten how it feels to be human."

The first inn they tried was the Turtle. The landlady studied them through a peephole. When she saw the giant, her eye vanished and the wooden bolt thunked into place. At the next inn they hid the giant out of sight until the landlady opened up. But no sooner had she caught a glimpse of him than she leaped back and slammed the door so hard that pots tumbled from shelves inside.

After asking at three more inns and having three more doors shut in their faces, sun going down, the deputies had all but resigned themselves to sleeping outside. As they passed a blacksmith's shop, the men who had been talking in the doorway fell silent and stared. The smith himself came out to see what had silenced them. In one fist he grasped a sledgehammer which ordinary men would hold in two. He slapped the hammer into his other palm as he looked the big man over. "Shoe those horses for you, mister?" he said, addressing the giant, even though the deputies were the ones sitting horseback.

"Their shoes are fine, sir," said Ely.

"You looking for work, big fellow?" The smith squinted up at the giant. "You maybe like a job with me bending wagon rims?"

"He ain't for hire, sir," said Ely.

"What do you say, big fellow?"

"I'm telling you he ain't for hire."

"Don't he talk for himself, son? He some kind of slave?" Appealing to the circle of wary listeners, the smith added, "Hey, boys, what do we think of slavery up here in Ohio?"

"He is most definitely not a slave," Owen put in quickly. "He is merely traveling under our protection. At the moment we're looking for a place to spend the night. We've tried the inns, without success. Would you have any suggestions?"

The smith took the giant's measure again, as if he had met so few men who were bulkier than himself that he could not get over the novelty. "You're welcome to sleep here in my stable."

"It is most kind of you, most kind," Owen said with relief. "The only other thing we could possibly need is a barbershop."

The smith pointed with the hammer. "Up at the next corner."

Owen turned to his partner. "Ely, would you mind terribly looking after our friend while I go visit that barber?"

"Sure, you go on. Get pretty."

The blacksmith and the other men stood back to let Ely and the giant pass through into the stable. Ely fed the horses and unfurled bedrolls onto the straw. The bearman squatted on his heels against the wall, showing no signs of hunger or weariness. When he could think of no more jobs to busy himself with, Ely sat down and began paring his fingernails. The bearman watched this operation through narrowed eyes. After Ely had finished and was putting his knife away, the bearman gave a grunt and thrust out his own broken-nailed paws.

Ely knew from the battle of wills in the cave that it was no use pretending not to understand. "Give it here, then," he said, taking one of the hair-backed mitts in his hand. The weight of it was like a horse's leg, and paring the horny nails was like trimming Babe's hooves. Afterward, the giant held both hands in the air and studied them admiringly.

"I don't know what name to call you," Ely said, certain his words fell on stone. It was not even clear how much sign language the giant could read. Ely's command of this hand talk was imperfect, just snatches picked up here and there. But he knew how to ask a person's name, and to this the giant would answer only with a blank stare. It was a good deal harder to ask him about the dwarf. Little ones who live under trees, Ely signed. Tiny man. Sells trinkets. Much money. You remember?

A faraway look came into the yellow eyes. Then with dreamlike slowness the giant began moving his fingers in the air: Girl. Water. Bird. Water bird?

"Rain Hawk?" Ely said aloud, signing the words back to him, and the giant wagged his great bearded jaw in agreement.

A dozen questions rushed to mind, but Ely could not think how to ask any of them in this clumsy speech of hands.

Smelling of pomade, clean-shaven, hair slicked back and shirt damp from a scrubbing, Owen returned to the stable with a hamper of food. "After a season of famine, Ely, my boy, it's time for a feast. We have here fried pork," he announced, spreading a neck scarf on the straw to serve as tablecloth, "corn dodgers, apples in molasses, wheat bread, melons, even maple sugar."

"And whiskey!" declared the smith, who followed him into the stable bearing two jugs, one hooked over each thumb.

Tears slithered down Owen's face as he ate. He sloshed the drink in his mouth, swallowing it a fiery sip at a time. The smith shoved an entire pork chop into his maw, chewed for a spell, and then withdrew the glistening bone. Between mouthfuls, Owen read items aloud from a newspaper he had purchased at the barber's. Corn prices were rising. Kentucky volunteers hoped to rout the British from Detroit before winter. Perry's fleet was preparing for a showdown with the British on Lake Erie.

Ely held the basket in front of the giant, but the bearded mouth would not open. The great hands lay still on his lap like slabs of woods. Maybe a drop of liquor will oil his jaw, the smallest drop, Ely thought, reaching out for a jug. But the smith grabbed his wrist and said, "No whiskey for Indians."

"He ain't any Indian," Ely snapped.

"If he ain't at least a half-breed I'll eat my boot."

Animated by the liquor, Owen bellowed, "He's the ninth wonder of the world, a marvel of nature!"

"I saw two fat ladies once in a fair," the smith recalled, "growed together at their bellies. How they slept or sat down was more than I could figure."

Owen lowered the jug with a gasp and thrust a finger in the air. "Ely, my boy, I see the road to our fortune. Let's chain him into a covered wagon and drive him through the countryside, charging fifty cents for a peek."

Ely spat a mouthful of biscuit on the straw. Back in the shadows the giant shifted with a heavy scraping of limbs against the wall.

"Paint SEE THE MONSTER on the side!" the smith suggested.

"Man-eater from Africa!" Owen declared.

"King of the barbarians!"

"Freak!"

The lawyer and the smith leaned on one another like wrestlers, heaving with laughter.

Furious, Ely ran outside, wishing the giant would murder them both, disappear, and this time leave no bootprints behind. In the alley he found a ring of children peering into the stable, their mouths wide enough to swallow boiled eggs. They peppered Ely with questions: "Is the giant gonna stand up, mister? Does he do tricks? How much does he weigh? How'd you catch him?"

"Shoo! Get along home with you!" Ely bawled at them. The children made way for him to pass through, then gathered behind him to gawk at the giant.

"What's he *eat?*"

"Children!" Ely called over his shoulder. Immediately he was sorry, for they took up the word, chanting, "Children! *Children!* He eats children!"

Ely crashed on into the night, jostling barrels and

late-walkers, past a knot of men cheering a cockfight, the birds gleaming with blood in the lantern light, past lounging soldiers, all the way running to the docks, where he stopped short, heart hammering, and tried to calm himself by watching the river's muscular gleam. If only he had lost the giant's trail, left him in that cave. Why had he stuck so doggedly to the hunt? There was no brother at the end of it, no marvel, only this overgrown child. Ely fingered the necklace at his throat, touched the spot on his forehead where the red paint had dried.

At length he knew he had to go back. What if the giant took it into his mind to leave? Would the black-smith beat him over the head with a hammer? Would Owen shoot him? He drifted back past the cockfight, past the loitering soldiers. As he broke through the huddle of children outside the stable he overheard one say, "I seen him eat a kid in each hand! He starts with the toes and chaws upwards!"

When he entered the lantern-lit shed he found the smith balanced on a crossbeam overhead, hands tucked in his armpits, crowing at the roof, shuffling chicken manure from the rafters with his feet. And Owen was loping around in circles below, kicking up his heels, coatless, vest unbuttoned, braces dangling. There was no sign of the bearman. Was he hiding in one of the stalls? Or run off? Dear God, let him be run off. Watching the smithy and the lawyer, Ely was filled with bitter memories of his father, roaring drunk, the cabin dizzy with the old man's rage.

Owen stopped his mad canter and braced himself

against a post. He thumped his belly and cried out, "No paunch anymore, my boy!" And it was nearly true; the chase had worn him down. There was straw in his hair, mud on his face. "Skin and bones! A true frontiersman! A man of the people!"

"Where is he?" Ely demanded.

Behind the glasses Owen's eyes looked like fertile eggs. Clinging to the post, he waved vaguely toward the rear of the stable. "Back with the other beasts."

From overhead, the smith called down, "No worry, boy. The girl's with him."

"What girl?" Ely turned his head sharply and stared back into the shadows of the stable.

Owen clutched his arm. In his eyes there was now an edge of soberness, like clear sky following a storm. "Ely," he said, "it's because I'm afraid. It's the fear makes me drink."

"Fear of what?"

"Fear it's all going to come crashing down."

"What's going to come crashing down?"

"Everything," Owen whispered, eyes widening. "Every last thing."

Ely jerked his arm free. "It's only liquor talking."

From his perch on the rafter the blacksmith cried, "No worry, son. I've got my eye on them. Ugly monster and pretty gal. Look in on them. It's a spectacle."

Ely took a lantern and made his way back to the stalls, and there he found the two of them, the huge bear of a man and the slight girl, black hair in braids, blue kerchief, shells swinging from her ears. The giant squatted and Rain Hawk stood feeding him pork and maple sugar bite-by-bite, breaking off chunks and slipping them into his patient mouth. They paid no heed to the blacksmith crowing or the lawyer lamenting, nor to Ely standing there amazed, but went silently on with their meal, the girl feeding, the great man chewing with the unhurried resolution of a bull.

11

Next morning the whiskey left Owen's head feeling as though it had served as a clapper in a church bell, yet he tried to reason with the girl. She would slow them down, he told her. "I ride my pony like the wind," she answered. But the trails would be a nightmare of mosquitoes and mud, he warned her. "I am not soft," she answered. It would be dangerous and awkward for her to travel with them, he pointed out, a lone girl with a boy and a man and a murderous giant. This brought a curl to her lips. "I do not fear anything that goes on two legs," she replied.

"If she means to come along," Ely muttered to him while they were packing the horses in the black-smith's stable, "there's no way to get shut of her unless we truss her up in rope."

So the four of them set out together. Children trailed them to the outskirts of Cincinnati, scurrying and jab-bering like a gaggle of geese until Ely shouted at them. The giant never looked round, not even when rocks thrown by the fleeing children thumped him on the shoulder.

They headed toward Chillicothe over what passed for roads. In places the trail was overgrown with sumac and crabapple, and elsewhere it petered out into creeks or led to the brink of cliffs. Still, by pushing hard, they made forty miles that day.

In camp, Rain Hawk groomed the giant's hair with a comb of bone, currying out the tangles, pinching the fleas between her nails. While she worked, the two of them kept up a constant chatter with gestures. Ely watched uneasily, because he could not follow most of what they were saying. The movement of their fingers was too fast, and too deeply Indian. Since discovering them at their silent meal in the blacksmith's shop, Ely had pestered the spice girl with questions: Why'd she come after them? How'd she know to look in Cincinnati? What the devil did she want with the giant? But for all the answers he got, he might as well have been talking to a fencepost.

When Ely played the flute, the giant perked up and leaned forward, head swaying to the melody. Rain Hawk began a sad, wordless crooning. The giant touched one hand to his ear, the other to his lips, and rocked in a bliss of listening.

Later, when the only singing was that of the locusts, Owen rolled over on his blanket and whispered to Ely: "Shouldn't we put him in irons? He might run away in the night, or strangle us in our sleep. I'm especially concerned for Mademoiselle Rozier."

"He ain't going to bother her," Ely whispered back. "Can't you see how she handles him? She could lead him around by a hair. I just wish I knew what she's got to do with him."

"We could chain him to a tree."

"If he had a mind to run off, he'd already have done it."

"I'd feel much better if he wore the manacles."

"You going to put them on?"

Owen remained silent a moment. "I see your point."

Ely propped himself on a bent arm. His joints felt sore, aguish. O Lord, he thought, let me not get sick. To Owen he whispered, "If he didn't kill that peddler, the judge will let him go free, won't he? That's what trials are for, ain't they? To see who's guilty and who's innocent?"

"That is the theory," said Owen.

"Well, then, all we got to do is deliver him safe, and the court will see to justice."

"The court will *look* for justice. What it will find is another question." Owen imagined twelve grim farmers in the jury box, worried about families and livestock. The judge in his powdered wig, bored, impatient, stopping briefly in Roma on his circuit of county seats, unable to read the giant's language of gesticulation. And crowding into the courtroom, filling the street outside, whispering in every corner would be the jittery townspeople. Guilt and innocence, innocence and guilt. Who could ever be confident of telling the one from the other?

In the morning Owen shuddered awake to find himself covered with green snakes. The giant, stooped over him, was peeling them off and flinging them into the woods.

"Best lie still until he's done," Ely said from the fire, where he was cooking breakfast. "They crawl on you for warmth. He's already slung away mine and Rain Hawk's. They ain't poisonous, but if they take a notion to bite you they'll swell you up big as a cow."

Owen lay still. He felt as if hair were growing inside his skull as well as out, needling into his brain. Above him the giant's face rose and fell like a bearded moon, with its trace of Indian in the cheekbones. The yellow eyes were intent upon the snakes, sparing Owen the discomfort of having to look into their alien depths. Hair the color of cinders stood out like a mane around the great head, making it seem even less human. When the last snake had been flung away, the giant began folding the blankets, which looked in those bulky arms like the rags used by girls for wrapping dolls. Leading this unchainable brute to Roma for trial seemed a more lunatic undertaking every time Owen thought about it. It made about as much sense as arresting a bear, and was about as safe. Better almost to shoot him now, or set him loose. Owen shook his head to clear it of such thoughts. That way lay savagery, the rule of blind force. Law, he reminded himself. Law law law. The only stay against barbarism.

Breaking camp was a slow business, because the girl insisted on praying before she would budge. But once she was mounted on her piebald pony, she rode hard, never complaining, scarcely eating, and the giant stalked along beside her. In the heat of the day, whenever they stopped to feed the horses, the giant gathered armloads of grass. Stripped to the waist and rivered with sweat, he seemed more akin to the horses than to people. At first the horses danced away from him, jerking at their reins with eyes rolled back. But soon they calmed beneath his touch, munching the grass he offered.

For three days they rode past cabins boarded up against Indians and stockades bristling with the barrels of guns. The settlers who showed themselves at all walked around like turtles, peering out from beneath shells of suspicion. They did not like the looks of the giant, or of the shabby deputies either, and they said so, escorting the party through town with guns. Nor did the spice girl soften their mistrust, for she wore a British soldier's coat of lobster red. "Where the devil did you come by that?" Ely had asked her. "My father killed the man who wore it," she had answered. Only the children in the villages seemed drawn to the giant. They leaked out of cabins from every cranny to peep at him through the crowd of armed men.

Upon leaving one of these villages, Owen said, "It's rather like traveling with a circus, the way everybody gawks at him."

Ely answered, "In Cincinnati you were saying we should chain him in a wagon and charge people to get a look at him."

"I said that?"

"With your own mouth."

"I'm afraid I made rather a fool of myself that evening."

"I won't quarrel with that, Mr. Lightfoot."

At night, wolves howled in the dark beyond the

campfire. Owen would have sworn there were more of them each evening, as if a troop had pursued them all the way from Cincinnati, gathering recruits along the way. After three nights of such howling, Ely awoke in the darkness to see the bearman padding away into the forest, quiet as the gliding moon. The trees swallowed the huge shape without a rustle. Ely sat up to mend the fire, but did not touch his gun, content to let the giant go.

"He will come back," murmured the spice girl.

Startled by the voice, Ely looked at the dark bundle where Rain Hawk lay, wrapped in the coat of a dead soldier. She sat up, and the firelight caught her teeth, her eyes, the shells dangling from her ears.

"How do you know?" Ely said. There was a fire in his joints. Fever coming. "You can't read his signs in the dark."

"I know by other signs."

"Has he got some kind of talk you can understand?"

"He does not speak with his mouth." Her own speech now was gentle, the sound of creeks over stone, nothing like that harsh crow voice she had flung at him through the walls of her hut.

"Has he got a name?" said Ely.

"He is called Bear Walks."

"And where does he come from? Who're his people?"

"He speaks of the north, where it is very cold and the snows are deep. Grandmother Canada? That is all he tells me. He has no memory. His mind is short like the grass."

"Does he know why we're taking him back to Roma?"

"The ways of white men are a mystery to him."

A mystery not only to him, thought Ely. He glanced at Owen, who snoozed beside the fire, head stuffed with books. Great lump of wheezing lawyer. "You told him about the jail and trial?"

"I told him."

"Then why don't he run off? I ain't going to shoot him."

"He does not understand. I have tried to lead him away. But he will not go." Her dark face tilted, color of tanned doeskin. The shells at her ears curved with firelight. "He will not leave you. Tree-Who-Sings, he calls you. His brother. How could his brother lead him to danger?"

There was no surprise in this for Ely, who had known as much since feeling the weight of the great man's arms wrapped about him in the cave. "I ain't his brother," he insisted.

"It is a great honor," said Rain Hawk.

"And what are you? His sister?"

Silence a moment. Then: "I am the bringer of his death."

"How do you figure that? You mean to kill him?"

"No." The beads on her dress made a harsh clacking.

"Then how're you bringing him death?" In her stubborn silence Ely remembered the two sets of bootprints leading to the hut, and the one set of huge prints leading away. "Are you saying he murdered the dwarf on account of you?" When she kept silent, he asked her a second time, a third, and still she would not speak. How could you make her talk? At length he said, "What's he after out there?"

"The wolves trouble him."

For a long while Ely sat without asking any more questions, poking at the fire, fingering the sharp teeth of his necklace. Presently the howling stopped, a hush fell over the woods, and the giant came padding into the firelight with a wolf draped across his shoulders. He laid his kill at Ely's feet—a gray wolf the size of a yearling calf, neck twisted awry, tongue hanging out like a leather strap. Ely made the sign for deep thanks, accepting this gift.

No amount of coaxing would persuade Owen to join the others in eating wolf for breakfast. Instead he made do with biscuits and dried apples.

Villages thickened in the neighborhood of Chillicothe, and so did the parties of armed men. Rumor said that British soldiers and Tecumseh's Indians were marching south into Ohio, aiming to burn the fort at Chillicothe and set free the war prisoners there and butcher everyone within a day's ride of the town. A light rain helped Ely persuade Rain Hawk to wear a blanket over her red coat. But there was no way of covering Bear Walks. Only the giant's beard kept him alive through that day, for no one had ever heard of an Indian with whiskers. Shaven, he would have been murdered for his high cheekbones and black shrub of hair. One farmer did take a shot at him. Ely swung round, drawing his own rifle, but the giant simply plodded onward at the spice girl's side, indifferent, unflinching.

"They are right to fear Tecumseh," said Rain Hawk. "He is a great warrior. Bullets will not pierce him."

"Is that a fact?" said Ely.

"Yes," she replied. "Nothing can kill him."

"How is it you know so much about him?"

"I come from his village. I played at his feet." There was the slightest tremor in her voice. "We always had much meat with Tecumseh there. Much singing and the sun shining."

"Why'd you leave, if it was so good?"

"They sent me away."

"Whyever for?" said Ely.

Rain Hawk turned her green gaze full on him. "Because I carry in me the poison of white blood from my father."

Shortly after sunset, in rain, they reached Chillicothe. Ely was thankful for the dark. He was feeling wrung out and woozy. They found the town encircled by tents made of linen sheets. Sentries paced back and forth across the road, tin cups stuck on their rifle barrels to keep out rain. Officers on horseback, with brass buttons glittering on their chests, sloshed around through the shadows. Damp soldiers glowered from tents as Ely guided his party toward the encampment. Somebody played a fiddle, the notes sounding gay in this mournful drizzle. Ely drew up shy of the sentry and kept the giant and spice girl beside him, sheltering beneath an ash tree in the dark, while Owen went forward to do the talking.

The fiddle kept on, squealing like a bird. The tune was one that Ely often played on his flute. How did the words go? His mind felt muzzy. It was a come-all-ye about a dying soldier—he remembered that much. Then a verse came to him, and he sang along with the fiddle:

> *But to our sad and sore surprise,*
> *We saw men like grasshoppers rise.*
> *"Freedom or death" was all their cry.*
> *Indeed, they were not afeared to die.*

Pausing to recollect another verse, Ely felt the giant's shoulder pressed against him, the shaggy head bent down close to listen.

"He wants you to keep singing," the spice girl murmured.

Tree-Who-Sings, thought Ely. With the bearman's wiry hair brushing his cheek, he sang all the verses he could remember. He was droning out the last line— "My wife and children shall mourn for me, whilst I lie dead in Amerikee!"—when Owen returned.

"This is the Chillicothe Cavalry Company," Owen reported. "They're leaving tomorrow for Sandusky, to join Harrison's forces. The colonel has given us permission to ride along with him as far as Columbus, and has offered us a tent for tonight."

Ely wrung water out of his cap, then slapped it back onto his head. "You told him about Bear Walks?"

"Yes, indeed. I gave him all the details."

"That makes it kind of official, don't it, folks knowing we got a man here charged with murder?" Feverish and dizzy, Ely stared at the dripping tents, the wagons heaped with gleaming barrels, the lanterns hung sputtering on stakes, and he wondered how something as boneless as a government a thousand miles away in Washington could muster an army here in the wilderness of Ohio. A government capable of showing that kind of muscle could surely hang a giant. He looked at Owen, feeling sick and weary right down to the bone. "Then I reckon we got to take him back."

Owen drew a blanket around his shoulders. "Were you thinking of setting him free?"

"I wasn't thinking anything."

The four of them had to circle round and round like dogs before they all found places to lie down in the tent. Ely ended up between the giant and the spice girl, shivering in his wet deerskin shirt and leggins. In the darkness he could hear Rain Hawk taking off her own wet clothes before wrapping herself in the dry blanket a soldier had given her. As he turned away, he caught a glimpse of her breasts rising like mounds of shadow, and for the first time since discovering the dwarf out front of her reedy hut, he quit thinking of her as a nuisance or a witch or a force of nature, and thought warmly of her as a girl. His teeth began to chatter. He knew he had a fever, but he could not tell which to blame for it, the chill from the rain or the presence of Rain Hawk lying naked in the blanket beside him. To keep himself from reaching out for her in dreams, he crossed his arms on his chest, trying to still the shivers. He groaned steadily in a lullaby voice, listening to the drizzle on the linen roof, and to the fiddle squealing with uncanny gaiety into the night.

When Ely came to, the bones felt loose in his joints

and his teeth rattled like musket-fire. He rose up muttering that he was not going to die of fever in this stinking hole, and if somebody didn't prop him on his horse in about half a minute he'd crawl there himself. When no one came to help, he lurched to his feet, then keeled over onto the dirt floor, where he lay shivering. The lawyer muttered nearby, and the spice girl cooed to him in Shawnee, but he could make nothing of it. Then he felt himself being lifted in two sturdy arms, rising limp and weightless as a rag doll, the way he had felt as a child when his father had carried him late at night from the houses of kinfolk to the family wagon. Not Pappy this time, Ely dimly realized through his fever—not Pappy but the giant was cradling him.

The tents of the encampment had already been folded, the cavalry had moved out with its herd of cattle bound for Sandusky, and the last wagons of the baggage train, escorted by a double file of sharpshooters, were just rolling onto the Columbus road.

"He cannot ride a horse," Rain Hawk told Owen.

Owen had already formed the same opinion, and was looking anxiously for some other means of conveyance. While he was debating, the giant lifted Ely onto the bed of a supply wagon, elbowing aside barrels and hemp sacks to make room. The driver glanced around at the commotion, puffing angrily at a pipe, ready to shout. Seeing the giant, however, he clamped his mouth shut and turned back to study the bony spines of his mules. The spice girl climbed aboard and took Ely's head in her lap.

And so they rolled into the morning, Ely rocking

feverishly among the barrels, certain he was dreaming the lovely green-eyed face that hung above him, the giant stalking beside him with one hand clamped to the wagon frame, and Owen trotting behind, leading the two spare horses, wondering how he would manage the ironman if his partner died.

12

FOR TWO DAYS IN THE WAGON AND FOR TWO INTER-
minable nights beside campfires Mademoiselle
Rozier kept watch over Ely, and Owen kept watch
over her, fearing she might run off at any moment
with the giant. The nights were the most agonizing.
Nodding off to sleep, Owen would dream that Ely
had died. Waking in a panic, he would find the giant
shoving wood onto the fire, hear the girl singing, and
see Ely lying deathly still, so still that Owen was afraid
to reach out and touch his wrist.

Wound in his blanket, Ely moved only to shiver.
The whites of his eyes were the color of mud. His
fingernails were blue. When chills shook him, the girl
held him close against her. She pressed damp cloths
to his forehead, fed him sips of broth she had brewed
from leaves, rubbed a pungent ointment on his chest.
The giant watched her, now and again emitting a grunt.
Owen felt certain that the simple brute, having come
along peacefully out of some animal loyalty to Ely,
was held there only by the sick boy's shuddering breath.
More than once, while trying to write in his journal,

Owen glanced up to find the giant staring at him, those yellow eyes glowing with the remote indifference of stars.

On the second night, when the army bivouacked just south of Columbus, Owen stole away to ask the commanding officer for the loan of a dozen soldiers to escort the giant back to Roma.

The officer stood beside a pit watching a pack of dogs fight a bear. His hair was tied in a ponytail with a thong. "I'll shoot him for you, if you'd like," he shouted above the snarling and yelling, "but I wouldn't loan you even a drummer boy to herd him anywhere else, not while this war is on."

"A wagon at least," Owen pleaded, "with a stout driver."

There was an uproar from the pit, where the bear had crushed a dog. "Positively not. Take my advice and shoot him now. Save the state the cost of trying him. And save your own neck."

Back in his own campsite, Owen cast about desperately for ways of delivering himself and the giant alive to Roma. All he could think of were the irons. But how to put them on? Perhaps the girl might help, for she appeared to exercise an authority over the giant second only to that possessed by Ely.

"Mademoiselle Rozier," Owen said to her that night, "would you mind telling me how you came to know the giant?"

"He has a name," she replied.

"I beg your pardon. I should call him Bear Walks. Is he a member of your tribe? A friend?"

"He is a stranger to me." She sat with Ely's delirious head in her lap, her fingers stroking his cheeks. The giant hunkered beside her. She corrected herself. "He *was* a stranger."

"Then why did you follow him?"

"It is what I had to do."

"But *why?*" The giant glared at him, with that starry indifference in his eyes, and Owen repeated more quietly, "Why?"

"First you say why you hunt him and lead him back to jail."

"You know quite well he is suspected of murder."

"Suspicion brings you all this way through the woods? A man like you who lives in chairs?"

Thinner, harder in the flesh, Owen was less bruised by her irony than he would have been a month earlier. "When someone is killed in my neighborhood, I can hardly turn my back and ignore it," he answered tartly. "In any case, the law is my profession. I am committed to upholding it in every way possible."

The girl startled him with a smile. "Then you know my reasons. The peddler died at my door, screaming like a rabbit. And now my own law tells me I must stay with Bear Walks."

"Did you see the murder?"

"I saw the little man die, yes."

Leading her gingerly on, Owen said, "And how did he die?"

There was a cold fury in her look. "I killed him."

This was nonsense, Owen felt certain. A stratagem to save the giant from hanging. He had seen the dwarf's mangled body. A sack of broken bones. No ninety-pound girl could have done that much damage. Indulging her, he said, "And how did you kill him?"

"With the power of my curse."

"Curse? What rubbish!"

Ely moaned. The girl whispered, "Quiet. Our talk stirs up his sleep." She trailed her fingers through the red mat of hair on his chest and drew loops around his eyes.

At daybreak the earth shuddered with the passing of the cavalry and its herd of beef. When Ely saw the ruddy face bent over him and the dark braids hanging down like ropes, he believed he was still wrapped in dream. But then Rain Hawk touched his cheek and said, "You have returned from the land of fire."

So the cushion beneath his head was truly her lap and the earthy smell was her actual smell. Lord, lord. To cover his confusion, he sat up and asked where in creation they were.

"Just south of Columbus," Owen replied with immense relief.

"Five days from Roma," Ely said. Swaddled in the blanket, he staggered to his feet, and promptly fainted dead away. The giant caught him, and again without asking permission loaded him onto the last wagon of the baggage train as it rolled from camp.

They soon found out why it was last. Every little while the driver would rein his oxen to a halt, leap to the road, and sling rocks at crows that roosted in sycamores along the river. The birds ignored him, scarcely ruffled a feather. When the other wagons disappeared around a bend, he would spring back onto his seat and lash the oxen in a frenzy to catch up. Having caught up, he would stop again at the next stand of crows. These halts and chases jarred every bone in Ely's body. So he made a sign to the giant, who strode forward and explained with his hands what would happen to the driver the next time the wagon halted. The wagon did not halt again before Columbus, but each time the driver passed a treeful of crows he gazed at it yearningly.

At Columbus, Ely managed to climb down from the wagon by himself. He leaned against Bear Walks as the army trudged on north toward the war. Encouraged by Ely's recovery, Owen sent the girl to buy food, then he himself slipped away to speak with a judge in the capitol about preparations for the trial.

On the northern edge of town, Ely settled down with the giant to rest in a clearing where men were raising a frame of logs. The men snaked treetrunks into the clearing with horses, hewed them square with axes, chopped notches and chamfers into the ends, and finally hoisted the logs into place. Ely admired their work. Holding onto the giant's arm for support, he shuffled over to ask what they were building.

"The state prison," one man answered, looking up from his work, the ax poised above a log. Noticing the giant, he added, "Why, you got call for one?"

Ely surveyed the length of the half-finished wall. "We need all that much prison just for Ohio?"

"It's on account of the riffraff that's come through with this war." The man drew a twig from his mouth and pointed at Ely and the giant. "Take you two, now—where'd you be from?"

"Up north by the lake."

"What you doing down here?"

"We're partners," said Ely. He leaned on the giant's arm, where he sensed the great pulse beating sluggishly.

"Partners doing what?"

Inexpert at lying, Ely said, "We're deputies," which was half true, "and we're chasing a murderer."

"Don't he talk? Is he foreign or something? Indian?"

"We're just fixing to leave," said Ely quickly.

"I heard about some big guy killed three people east of here," said the man with the chewed twig. "You hear about that?"

"No, I sure haven't," Ely said, tugging at the giant.

"Why don't he talk? What's wrong with him?"

"We got to go." Ely pulled at the thick arm in which the blood hammered now. Finally the giant turned, yielding to his pull, and shambled away.

"You go, and you keep on going!" one of the axmen shouted.

By the time Owen and Rain Hawk caught up with the pair, they were halfway to Zanesville. Ely was clinging to the saddle horn with both hands while the giant led the mare by her bridle.

"Our friend threw quite a scare into Columbus," said Owen as he rode abreast. "Word of him reached the courthouse while I was having dinner with the judge. Whatever did he do?"

"He just stood there and let them have a gander at him," said Ely. "That's all it took."

Rain Hawk rode on her black-and-white patchwork

pony within arm's reach of Ely. "How do you feel?" she said.

"Good enough to keep on riding." Even while speaking, Ely never let go his grip on the saddle horn. "But that's the worst I ever had the fever." He swayed, and the giant put a bracing hand against his ribs. "Tell me this, Mr. Lightfoot," said Ely. "Instead of hanging him, could the judge send him to that new prison they're building in Columbus?"

"Is it really wise to speak of this in front of him?"

"Why not?" Ely stroked the black head, the stiff hair like pine needles. "You don't understand about courts and hanging, do you, friend?" The giant turned on him those yellow eyes, not so much looking at him as presenting his face for study, the way a child will show a forehead where cuts have healed. Ely wondered what stirred there, behind that forehead as wide as a bucket.

To the girl, Owen said, "But you seem to be able to make him comprehend a great deal, Mademoiselle Rozier."

"Not with words. He has no words."

"With your hands, then."

"With my hands, yes, I can speak of sleep and food and the path. I can make him understand what is in front of his nose. But I cannot tell him about yesterday or tomorrow."

"He doesn't have any memory," said Ely.

"Or any imagination, it would seem," said Owen. Perfectly like a beast, locked in the present moment. Could such a brute be either guilty or innocent? While talking with the circuit judge in Columbus, Owen had in fact raised the very question that Ely just now put to him. "We might get him sent to the penitentiary," he said, "on the grounds of mental incompetence."

"Meaning—on account of he's an idiot?" said Ely.

"That's the rough meaning, yes."

"I don't know." Ely fanned himself with his hat to keep off mosquitoes. "I hate to think of him penned up in there for years, always stooped over, and everybody who looks at him thinking he's some kind of freak. Better almost to hang him."

"Or let him return to the woods," Rain Hawk urged. "Send him far away to the north where no white men go. In the woods away beyond peddlers and soldiers and the stink of towns."

Stung by her words, Ely said, "How do you figure getting him to wander off into the backcountry and stay there?"

"He would follow wherever you lead him. Even to the ocean, to the lands of snow, to the mountains at the end of the world." She reached out a hand to grasp Ely by the shoulder and steady him in the saddle, for he was feeling woozy again. "And wherever you stay, he will stay there with you."

"Despite what Mademoiselle Rozier says, and despite what you may feel," Owen advised his partner, "I would not trust too completely in your ability to control the ironman."

"I'd just as soon quit talking about it," said Ely.

They were camped near Zanesville, beside the Muskingum. Rain Hawk was down bathing in the river, crooning her Shawnee songs. She was out of sight beyond a clump of willows, but that did not keep Ely's thoughts from circling round her wet body. The giant squatted beside the campfire, cracking the bones of a roasted rabbit and sucking the marrow.

"The peddler must have acquired the same hold over him," said Owen. "How else could he have per-suaded the big man to carry that rucksack from Pitts-burgh, and to walk up to cabins in the woods and terrify housewives into buying trinkets?"

"Don't go on about it," said Ely.

"It's as though he had the creature mesmerized. A trained animal he could manipulate any way he liked." Owen glanced at the hulking prisoner. He could not forget how those yellow eyes had gazed at him with starry indifference over the feverish body of Ely the night before. "But remember how the giant turned on the peddler and jammed him into that stump."

"And you remember," said Ely, separating his words for emphasis, "that he'll do any sweet little thing I tell him."

Owen gave a bitter laugh, recalling how the coun-try woman had stood in his office, hands twisting in her skirt, and had quoted those very words from the dwarf. Seeing the cold set of Ely's face, however, he stopped laughing. "Don't even joke like that," he said nervously.

The girl returned at that moment from her bathing, a sheen of moisture on her face and throat. Around each eye she had drawn a white circle with clay, giving her the look of an owl. She sat by the giant and wrung water from her thick hair.

Satisfied that she was not listening to them, Owen hissed at Ely: "You *were* joking, weren't you—about sicking him on me?"

Ely dredged phlegm from his throat, then spat. "I was joking. I don't want him hurting nobody, least of all you. That's what I want to stop—folks hurting folks."

"I didn't find it amusing," said Owen.

"It was a crazy thing to say." Ely watched Rain Hawk braiding her wet hair. Her eyes, in the painted circles, seemed to glow like green foxfire. "I guess I'm all a mess of feelings about leading him back this way. Sometimes I say fool things."

Owen's fear drained away and in its place he was surprised to discover a feeling of tenderness for his moody, exasperating partner. Leaning close, to shield his revelation from the girl, he confided, "It's just possible we might get him set free. Provided, of course, you deliver me in one piece back to Roma."

"What's you being in one piece got to do with it?"

Owen delayed answering for a moment, savoring his secret. He was finally beginning to understand what Ely suffered. Here was a boy who had ridden out on the trail of a monster, lured on by the challenge of facing down some marvelous beast—and what had he captured? How much honor was there in this conquest over a trusting idiot? At last Owen whispered, "If I'm in one piece, I can do a much better job of defending him at the trial."

Ely gave him an amazed look. "You're going to speak up for him in court?"

"In Columbus I arranged with the judge to serve as defense attorney. He'll bring his own prosecutor with him when he comes through Roma on his circuit next month."

"You mean, after chasing Bear Walks from one end of Ohio to the other and dragging him back for trial you'll try to get him set free?" Confounded yet again by the lawyer, Ely raked fingers through his hair. "That's crazy. That's pure-dee *crazy.*"

"Where else would he turn for help?"

Ely thought about the town's dread of the big-footed man, and about the risk Owen would take by speaking up for him. This needed a kind of courage, too. Not the sort that made a man crawl into a pitch-black cave, maybe, but it was still courage. "That ain't going to help your business in Roma any."

"Probably not," Owen agreed.

"It might ruin you in that town."

"Indeed it might."

For the first time since dumping the dwarf on Owen's desk, Ely looked directly at the man, past eyeglasses and store-bought suit. "Why would you do a fool thing like that?"

"It's my profession. The law is all I have."

Something in his desolate tone reminded Ely of that drunken raving back in the blacksmith's stable. "What did you mean in Cincinnati, with all that whiskey in you, when you said how you were afraid everything was going to come crashing down?"

Owen thought of possible explanations, but he

doubted any of them would make sense to Ely. He shrugged. "It was just drunken nonsense."

In the dark, the giant began whistling through one of the hollow rabbit bones.

For three days more they journeyed north, avoiding towns. Rain Hawk straddled her pony like a man, skirts drawn up to her knees. After each night's bath in the river she added a few white strokes to the design painted on her forehead and cheeks, making her look even more owlish and forlorn. The giant kept up with the horses effortlessly, now and again blowing through his rabbit bone as a sign that he wanted Ely to play the flute.

The deputies spoke freely now before him, and before the girl, who seemed oblivious, wound up in her own private grief. They talked about the upcoming trial, about Roma, about their two fathers, about the war and the settlement of the land, and the more they talked, the more painfully they recognized their differences. Ely wanted the land left raw; Owen wanted it settled. Ely cared little for the company of people, liked being alone, while Owen needed crowds, streets, brick walls.

From a hill north of Zanesville they could see ridge after forested ridge stretching away toward Lake Erie. For hundreds of square miles there was nothing visible but trees. Roma was buried among those ridges somewhere, and so were other brand-new villages. Knowing the view of unbroken forest was an illusion, Ely still took pleasure in it. He enjoyed thinking that folks might have abandoned Roma, gone back east of the mountains; maybe there would be no one left to hang the giant.

The nearer they drew to Roma, the more slowly Ely rode. He kept dismounting to lead his mare, to drink from creeks, to study the bark of trees. The giant dogged patiently after him, touching the same trees, slurping water from the creeks, shadowing his every move. Ely found each mile painful, as if he were climbing over and over again that steep cliff to the cavemouth. And still, although moving at a crawl, on the twenty-eighth night of the hunt they slept within a dozen miles of Roma.

The sun never seemed to rise on that last morning of the journey. Fog hung in gullies, and what little sky showed through the trees was the dull gray of gunpowder. Long after Owen had packed and saddled Blackstone, and Rain Hawk had finished her prayers and climbed onto her pony, Ely still sat cross-legged on a mound of leaves, at first braiding a new band for his hat from strips of cattails, and then doing nothing at all, only resting there with shoulders adroop and hands upcurled in his lap. Fog rose from the gullies and spread through the forest while Owen fidgeted. Standing behind Ely, the giant loomed out of the mist, as motionless as if he were a tree rooted there.

"We have to go, partner," Owen said gently. "The trial date is set. They're expecting us to bring him in."

"I know," Ely said.

The girl spoke: "Do not rush him. He must prepare himself."

For a long while Ely said nothing. Then, uncurling his hands so they lay palms up on his thighs, he said,

"We been having to go ever since I touched that dwarf." He ran his fingers over the necklace of bear teeth, tracing each sharp bone. "He don't fit, he just don't fit anywhere. There's no room left in the woods."

Owen peered up through the trees at the leaden scraps of sky. The whole country seemed raw to him, inhuman, cruel. The air seeping into his lungs was damp with the vapors of an earth that had nothing to do with man. He could sense Ely identifying with the giant and with these wilds, but he could not see how to prevent it, to save him.

At last Ely heaved himself upright, slapped the damp leaves from his breeches, and mounted the waiting mare. Once in motion, he stopped neither to drink nor eat nor rest, but rode grimly on.

The four of them burrowed into the shadowy day, fog settling on the lawyer's spectacles, on the girl's painted face, on Ely's fiery hair and the giant's beard. North of Canton they joined a horse trail, narrow in Ely's memory, but trampled wide now by militias passing to and from the fort at Cleveland.

At mid-morning they had to leave the trail and beat their way across wooded country. They soon heard axes thudding against trees. Rain Hawk drew rein, and waited at a distance with the giant while the deputies rode on to meet the axmen, a father and six sons who were cutting a road from Roma. The father was Bridsey Summers, known to Owen as a tenacious schemer who would stop you in the road and draw with a stick in the dust grandiose plans for canals and highways.

"Owen Lightfoot!" Summers hollered. "We all

thought you and the boy was dead and gone. My, you look wore down to a frazzle."

"It's us in our skins," said Owen, who could feel himself looking tattered, worn, transfigured in the man's eyes.

The sons leaned on their axes, grouped around the father like six younger versions of him, all bony, all with the eyes of dreamers. Summers asked, "That giant fellow give you the slip, did he?"

"No, indeed," said Owen.

"Did you shoot him?"

"Certainly not."

First one and then another of the sons noticed the huge man, who was hunched down warily behind the spice girl's pony. One of the sons gave a whistle, and the giant stood up.

"God almighty!" the father swore. "Will you look at that!"

"We promised to bring him back," said Ely harshly, "and we brung him back. Now let us by so we can get him on into town."

The father and sons made way, tightening the grip on their axes when the giant stalked by, seven pairs of eyes looking back over the stumps and downed logs and heaped brush of the road they had cut, as the lawyer and the boy, along with the painted squaw and the great shambling man, vanished into the fog toward Roma.

13

Thunder boomed north of them over Lake Erie, making the sky seem cavernous, as the deputies and the giant and the spice girl rode into Roma. No one ventured from the crouching cabins to meet them, not even children. In the graveyard were five heaps of freshly turned dirt. Planks had been nailed crisscross over doorways. Around the square, carts and wagons stood heaped with household goods—blankets, bedsteads, grandfather clocks, feather ticks, churns, spinning wheels. Horses and oxen and even a few miserable cows stood in yokes, swatting flies with their tails, waiting. In the boarded cabins, shadows moved behind the windows of greased paper, but no one stuck so much as a face outdoors.

Owen felt betrayed. Roma seemed to have died while he had been out hunting the giant, as if the villagers had simply given up the struggle against weather and epidemics and beasts and Indians, and had decided collectively—the way migrating birds will swerve with a single inclination—to move back east. They had

[155]

packed the town onto wagons, and in a few hours, from the looks of things, there would be no citizens left to form a jury, no jailer to guard the ironman, no county seat to host the trial.

"You reckon it's the war?" Ely asked.

"It could be any number of things," Owen said. "There's no shortage of plagues and disasters out here."

Rain Hawk startled them both with a rapid shake of her head, which set her ornaments of shells and beads to clacking. "No, it is the curse on the land."

Beneath Ely's outstretched hand, the giant's shoulder flexed, tightened; the muscles under the buckskin shirt felt like rock under moss. "What are we going to do with him?"

Thunder boomed again and again in the north.

"It might mean returning him to Columbus for trial," Owen replied. The town, his law practice, dreams of becoming a naturalist, everything had been stolen from him while he chased this monster, and even now he was not free of the dumb beast. The creature returned his look of loathing with one of utter indifference, blinking lazily. Owen added, "Perhaps I should have let that militia officer shoot him."

Ely turned fiercely on him. "No, you wouldn't either, you'd never let anybody shoot him, Mr. Lightfoot, because you're a man of the law, and no one's proved he's guilty of anything except being big and dumb. Ain't you a man of the law?"

"I try to be." Owen knew his own weakness, but found himself stretching to fit Ely's picture. "Don't you worry, I'll get him a fair trial if I have to deliver him to Washington."

Catching sight of a face skulking in the door of the livery stable, Ely cried, "Mr. Spinks, is that you? Ho, Mr. Spinks!"

Jonas Spinks limped from the stable, dragging his crippled leg. "We'd about give up looking for you two ever coming home," he said. "Nobody figured you'd catch up with him, never mind bringing him back." He circled the giant the way he circled any new horse brought to his stable, wary and bold at the same time. The giant did not even look at him. "Is he tame?" Spinks asked.

"No, he ain't altogether tame," Ely said. The word sounded in his ears like the cruelest name a man could be called. "But if you mean, is he dangerous—I don't think so. He hasn't give us a minute's trouble since we caught him."

Spinks backed away anyhow, sensing in the great man a force more lethal than the kick of a mule. Taking notice of the spice girl, he said, "Who's your friend here?"

Owen said, "Surely you know Mademoiselle Rozier."

Spinks peered at her. "Why, so it is. I'd never have recognized you, ma'am, behind all that paint."

With great dignity, she turned her face away. Ely wanted to wrap his arms around her and ease her grief, as she had eased his fever. He knew she was as tightly bound to Bear Walks as he was himself, although he had only the glimmering of a notion why.

Owen asked, "Jonas, what's happened to Roma since we left?"

"All the men are fighting up around Detroit. They

left right after you did, every able man except the Summers boys, who're chopping a road for the army, and me, who's a lame piece of goods." As if to prove his right to remain behind, Spinks hobbled in another circle around the giant.

The deputies stared north, where thunder still rolled.

"A man rode in here last night," Spinks continued, "and said they was fixing to be a big fight of ships on the lake today. Said if Perry's boats lost, the British were going to march down this way with a bunch of Tecumseh's savages and burn us out, and if we knew what was good for us we'd best light out for Pittsburgh." Spinks waved an arm at the loaded wagons. "So all the women and children and old men are hid indoors, waiting for a rider to come by and tell us how the battle turned out."

Ely and Owen listened afresh to the thunder.

"Cannon," Spinks said. "Been booming like that for about an hour. It's a wonder any of them ships's still afloat."

The deputies said nothing, sitting on their horses amid the loaded wagons. Owen could imagine the cabins tumbling apart into logs again, the logs reverting into trees, so that anyone passing through here two days hence would find nothing but forest.

"Might as well bring your horses on inside," Spinks offered.

The deputies swung down and followed him into the stable. Rain Hawk did not dismount until Ely spoke to her one of the two dozen Shawnee words he knew, which was simply, "Come."

While the deputies told about the hunt, the spice girl fed corn to her piebald pony, and the giant walked among the horses in the dark stalls. Spinks watched the huge man closely.

"He won't hurt a thing," Ely said.

But the liveryman listened uneasily to the horses nickering and the heavy feet shuffling.

"Did the sheriff go off with the militia?" Owen inquired.

Spinks nodded. "They'd have been better off taking his wife. She's got the jail key, if that's what you're after." He kept craning about to follow the giant's movements in the depths of the stable. "What's he *doing* back there?"

"I'm telling you, he won't hurt a thing," Ely said.

Just then a hoof thudded against a board in one of the stalls. Spinks seized a pitchfork and headed into the shadows, saying, "He's killed one of my horses." Ely did not bother to grab him. In a few moments Spinks returned, the pitchfork handle in two pieces, the color drained from his face. "You get him out of here. Lock him up. Get him out of here right now."

Ely went back into the gloomy stable. He reappeared shortly, holding the giant by the sleeve.

"Lock him up good and tight!" Spinks called after them, as the deputies led their captive into the street. Rain Hawk lurked along some paces behind them, a furtive shadow.

The log jail rose two stories, with an upstairs for the sheriff's family and downstairs for criminals. Mrs. Jenkins met them in the doorway, her face pinched tight. Ely touched the giant's elbow, stopping him a few paces short of the entrance.

"I heard you talking with Jonas," she announced. "There's food in the cell, and a mattress."

"We can see to locking him in," Ely said. He didn't want anybody to watch him abandon this creature, who had never once abandoned him since giving him that necklace back in the cave.

"What's that awful stench?" Mrs. Jenkins asked.

"What stink?" Ely could no longer distinguish the bearman's smell from his own. "Us, I expect."

"And what about her?" Mrs. Jenkins nodded at the spice girl, who was standing motionless a few paces away, the blue headscarf ablaze with sun, the white designs on her face gleaming. "Is she to be locked up as well?"

"No, ma'am," Ely insisted, "she's just interested."

"Interested," Mrs. Jenkins echoed the word contemptuously. She cast a long appraising look at the giant. Her face seemed worn past fear, like the face of a child who has cried past tears. "Pray God the men will come home soon, and all this"—she waved at the town square where other women had resumed the loading of wagons—"all this nightmare will come to an end." She handed Ely the key, which was as long as a pistol barrel, then climbed back up the stairway to her bedroom over the cell.

Would she be able to sleep up there tonight, with that creature rummaging about in the jail beneath her? Owen thought of Mrs. Forbes. Was she alone in her cabin, waiting like everyone else to hear the messenger ride hallooing through town with news of the battle? Sensing that Ely would not want him along to watch the locking-up, Owen said, "Do you need any help?"

"No, you go on ahead," said Ely. "But if you ain't got nothing else to do, you might take Rain Hawk back to your place."

"Actually, I had thought of paying my respects to Mrs. Forbes," said Owen. Ely stared at him, unrelenting. Owen sighed. "Very well. Mademoiselle Rozier?" But when he turned to look for her, wondering how Mrs. Forbes would feel about sharing his company with the girl, she was nowhere to be seen.

"Where in blazes is she gone to now?" said Ely. "It's like she's a *real* hawk. Flies here, there, and not a sound."

Relieved, Owen said, "Doubtless she'll turn up," and headed for his rendezvous with Mrs. Forbes.

The giant padded into the jail behind Ely, down the hall past cider barrels and mounds of carded wool. The cell door hung open. Your house here, Ely explained in gestures. Home. Sleep. Eat. The giant had to stoop in order to enter his cage. Food lay in willow-ware dishes on the floor—cold stew and boiled potatoes and johnnycakes. The big man crouched over the plates, waiting until Ely nodded at him, and then he wolfed the food.

The cell was cluttered with harness, barrel staves, a churn; drifts of fleece matted with dung; a crock full of pickles in brine; hoop poles that had been water-bent and were curing; dry gourds that rattled and green ones that lay heavy in the hand; sacks of feathers and three brooms worn to a nub; so much gear in fact that Ely had to clear a space for the giant to lie down. The room smelled of leather and disuse. Sweat burned Ely's eyes. He felt cramped, smothered, watching the great man stoop over. Sit, sit, Ely gestured, pointing to a three-legged stool. It collapsed, dropping the giant onto the cornhusk pallet, where he sat spraddle-legged like an enormous child at marbles.

Stay, Ely gestured. Sleep. The giant looked up at him with that inexpressive face while Ely backed toward the door. Drawing the key from his shirtpouch, the metal bone-cold against his fingers, he remembered how that face had loomed over him during the fever, the shaggy head outlined against the sunset like a tree. How to say in sign language, *I am betraying you?* All he could do was speak aloud: "I'm sorry, it's the law, you've got to stay here." Words seemed as futile now as before. Those eyes, yellow and blank as a cat's, watched him go.

Through the peephole Ely could see the great man sitting there, so motionless that the cornshuck mattress did not rustle, his bulky shoulders hunched forward, his great wolf-killing paws lying abandoned in his lap, his eyes fixed on the door. Ely drew a last breath of the stale air, air saturated now with his own and the giant's presence. Then he turned the key in the lock.

In the street, loaded wagons bulked around him like grazing buffalo. Eyes watched him through gaps in cabin walls, as if, having touched the giant, Ely had taken on some of his menace. Here and there stealthy figures lashed one more pot or shovel to the carts. He had to remind himself that this was Roma. He also had to remind himself that the thunder he kept hearing was cannon fire, grown sporadic now, so impossibly far away and feeble that it seemed to rattle in another world. A bitter homecoming: Instead of feeling relieved of a great weight, he felt burdened, powerless to move forward or to shed his load, like the motionless wagons chocked in the street.

After a mad final clashing the cannon fire ceased. Women crept outside to listen. But no more thunder followed, no more shooting. Within a few hours they would know who had won the battle. Everyone feared it would be the British, who had had things pretty much their own way since the war's beginning. The women already felt the long ache in their joints from the ride to Pittsburgh, already heard the wails of exhausted children.

What I ought to do now is take off, Ely thought. Shake the dust of this place from my feet. But he could not snap the cord that bound him to the giant, and so for hour after hour he circled through the watchful town, round and round again over his own path as if staked to the jail by rope.

Finally he stopped before the lawyer's office and gazed in through the window. Owen sat writing at his desk, which was covered with the law's mysterious papers, just as it had been on the morning when Ely staggered in carrying the dwarf. He remembered the crowd watching Owen count the money, Rain

Hawk standing on a chair to see, her midnight hair in braids, eyes like scraps of meadow, blue rag on her head like a patch of sky. Ely knew he shouldn't barge in now, but a longing to talk with the man who had shared the hunt with him overcame his reluctance, and in he went.

After finishing a sentence, Owen looked up. "Did it take all this while to lock him up?"

"Naw, I just been killing time." Ely drooped into a slat-backed chair. The slats cut into his spine. "I never did see Rain Hawk. You find everything all right with Mrs. Forbes?"

"As well as could be expected in these dismal times," Owen replied. In fact it had taken all of his out-of-practice charm to coax her into speaking with him. A badly frightened woman, Mrs. Forbes might never forgive him for having abandoned her. He studied his moody partner. It hurt him to see the boy so wrung out. "You can't have enjoyed that very much, shut-ting him away."

Ely nodded, and left his chin resting on his chest, too weary to face the lawyer, yet drawing comfort from this man whom he had despised a month earlier. From the smell of pomade and fresh linen, he knew Owen had bathed and changed clothes, had washed the trail from his body. But still the trail lay inside them both, the hoofbeats and the river and the cave. There was no washing that away. "It wouldn't be so hard if I only knew what he was," Ely said. "He's too strong and dumb for a man, too smart for a beast. We wouldn't hunt a bear or panther as hard as we hunted him. But if he was a man, he wouldn't have come along with us all peaceable like he did, back here to a jail and rope."

"So far as the law is concerned, he is a man, and will have to stand trial for murder."

"But I doubt he even remembers it. Whenever I try to make him understand 'peddler' or 'dwarf,' he just makes his sign for Rain Hawk."

Owen had often wondered what dim link existed in the brute's mind between the two, and why Mademoiselle Rozier claimed so implausibly that she, such a wisp of a girl, had killed the dwarf. Obscure sympathies—beasts and savages. "Ely," he said, "we did what we had to do. How are people ever going to live in this country without slaughtering one another, unless we bring murderers to justice?"

"I know, I know," Ely muttered.

After a few moments of silence the lawyer's quill began scratching again, persistent as the sound of mice in a corncrib. The mere act of writing, never mind what language he wrote, set him apart from Ely, who sat waiting for some release from the burden of this giant. The quill scratched through minute after minute, moved onto a new sheet of paper. The clean boiled shirt and velvet tie and gold-rimmed spectacles still looked ridiculous on the lawyer. But Ely now knew too much about the man inside them to feel contempt. Finally he asked, "They'll hang him, won't they?"

Owen glanced up, his mind still laced into his writing. "Not if I can help it. That's what I'm working on, a way to keep him alive."

"Well, go on. I'll just sit here like a possum and watch."

Owen pared a new turkey quill and resumed his writing. For a few minutes Ely watched the black lines snake across the paper. The law coiled out through Owen's fingers, twirled out inky and indecipherable to entangle the giant and draw him into that paper world where Ely was powerless to follow.

The way the lawyer bent over his paper reminded Ely of the giant hunched over in his cell. "You know, he won't even be able to stand up again until they haul him outside for the trial."

Owen swiveled around with a look of impatience that gave way to one of consternation. Pointing toward the door, he said, "Guess who's come to visit."

Ely turned to see the giant peering through the glass door, ATTORNEY arched in gold across his chest, the rabbit bone whistle stuck between his lips.

"Them blasted cheap-jack hinges," Ely swore. The giant must have burst from the cell, like a child shattering a basket, and then sniffed after him to the lawyer's office. Ely rose with a groan. "Come on, big fellow. Let's get you back to jail."

"Perhaps you could stay with him," Owen suggested, "at least until we learn the outcome of the battle, or until we get the door mended."

"Maybe I'd better," Ely agreed, hearing the lawyer's voice grow formal again, as if, back among his books, Owen put on the stuffy voice like a starched shirt. Ely was on the point of asking what to do with the giant in case Perry lost and the British invaded, but he kept mum, deciding he had already done enough to honor justice. If Roma died tonight, he would set the giant free.

Owen resumed his mouselike, mysterious scratching.

Outside, the giant began whistling through the hollow bone. "So you want a song, do you?" said Ely, touching his lips and ear. He launched into "Derby Ram": "As I went down to Derby, all on a market day, I met the biggest ram, boys, that ever fed on hay," only realizing when he reached the chorus why this gay song had leaped to mind:

> *And didn't he ra-a-mble, ra-a-mble,*
> *He rambled all around, in and out of town,*
> *He rambled till them butchers cut him down.*

The giant kept whistling for more, but that was all Ely felt like singing.

In the hallway leading to the cell, Ely tripped over buckets and spinning wheels. The giant shuffled quietly behind, kicking nothing, as sure in the dark as a panther. The plank door lay flat, ripped from its hinges. In the murk of the cell Ely glimpsed the designs of white paint, like ghostly writing, a moment before Rain Hawk spoke.

"He whined for you," she said. "I listened outside the window, and he kept whining for you after you left."

Just like a hawk, thought Ely. Flies back in here to roost. "Where you been?"

"Talking with the spirits."

"You figuring to stay in here with me and him?"

"There is room."

Then he noticed that all the trash and goods had been removed from the cell. Already she had laid claim to the place, made it a nest. "Do as you please," he said.

Nothing remained of the giant in the gloom except the bellows breathing. That was enough to keep Ely's sense of guilt alive while he stood at the window, hands poked through the wooden lattice, waiting for the rider to bring news of war from Lake Erie. The town waited around him, alert in the darkness. Men he knew would be hugging rifles up north, fretting about their wives and children here in Roma. Let Perry win, Ely thought. Let the town survive. But a voice in him was also pleading: Let Perry lose, let the British invade, let the giant live. He felt ashamed, wishing for fire and blood to sweep over Ohio; but the desire lingered.

Verses of "Derby Ram" kept swirling in his head:

The man who butchered this ram, boys,
Was drownded in the blood,
And the boy that held the basin
Was washed away in the flood.
Took all the boys in our town to roll away his bones,
Took all the girls in our town to roll away the stones.

Hours later a horn sounded far to the north, so faintly at first that it might have been a dog baying, then more loudly as it neared Roma, belling through the darkness. Ely could hear the whine of the messenger's cry long before he could make out what the man was shouting. Rain Hawk stirred. Even the giant woke to the sound of the horn. Ely sensed him rising to peer through the window, and he wondered how to make the wordless creature understand what this shouting meant.

"Victory!" the messenger cried. "Perry's won! Perry's won!"

"The soldiers will be coming home?" Rain Hawk whispered.

"They'll be coming home," said Ely.

After the hoofbeats died away, carrying news of Perry's victory deeper into Ohio, Ely heard the giant lie heavily down again on the cornshucks, and in the street he heard the scrape of furniture being dragged from wagons.

14

EIGHT DAYS LATER A RAGGED BAND OF ROMA militiamen trooped home from the war, coated with dust and pride. From the sidewalk in front of his office, Owen watched them come. Their swaggering made the powder horns and bullet pouches swing dizzily from their shoulders. Rubbing lips clean with the backs of wrists, the men kissed their wives and tossed their children squealing into the air. Sons fingered the tomahawks and hunting knives in their fathers' belts. Daughters stood aside combing snarls from their hair with fingers, waiting for hugs, anxious to see which soldiers had not come home. When the survivors named those who had died, the unhusbanded and unfathered began to wail.

Catching sight of Owen, one of the men called boisterously, "Lawyer, good to see you made it back! Where's Ely Jackson at? We've got news for him that'll make him dance!"

"I believe you'll find him in the jail!" Owen shouted.

"Jail? What's that rascal done?"

"He's looking after our prisoner."

"Prisoner? You *caught* him? That murdering giant?"

The man accused of murder, Owen thought, but he made no answer. It was vulgar to be shouting in the street like a mule driver, while all around him husbands and wives embraced and grieving women wailed. What news for Ely? News to make him dance. He remembered Ely on the flatboat, beside campfires, dancing upon his hands, legs lolling in the air. Owen withdrew into his office, the shrieks of new orphans and widows ringing in his ears.

Seated at his desk where the peddler's corpse had lain only five weeks earlier, he felt as though he had suffered rather more like five years' worth of change. Since returning he had not been able to rouse Mrs. Forbes from her dazed lassitude. She kept house for him as before, and cooked his meals, but she did so languorously, hair snarled like a rat's nest, dress half-buttoned, unpainted face as pale as chalk. Even her speech, once a reassuring primness in his ears, was now slurred and halting.

During his absence she had dutifully gathered stories about other settlers, all of them women, who had been terrorized by the dwarf and giant. There were half a dozen cases in Pilgrim County alone. At each cabin the peddler had forced the women to buy his trinkets, threatening to sic the giant on anyone who refused. "He made them surrender every penny they had in their houses," explained Mrs. Forbes, "and then he whistled to the giant and went away." In these stories of women pushed beyond the limits of endurance, Mrs. Forbes heard again and again her own story.

While the militiamen whooped it up outside, Owen

gazed absently at the stack of handwritten pages before him, unable to focus his mind on the argument he had spun so carefully. Noises from the street warned him that legal argument might well be futile, anyway. These men had fought too hard against distant enemies to shy away from killing one who turned up in their own village, and the women had faced too much fear in their boarded cabins to feel pity for an overgrown brute with the capricious mind of a child. Eventually, the shrieks of those who had lost fathers or husbands retreated indoors, became private grief.

Mulling over what to do about the trial and about Mrs. Forbes, Owen felt a keen thirst for whiskey. There was a flask of Pig and Whistle in his desk, just an arm's reach from his lips. But he resisted the temptation. Since making a fool of himself in Cincinnati, he had touched no liquor at all. What he had long assumed to be a perennial background fog in his mind had lifted, and he was beginning to see himself, his ambitions, and this town in a starker light. Ely's storybook image of him as the upholder of justice had affected him, it seemed. And although he still lived in horror of chaos, he refrained from dissolving that horror in alcohol.

"Ely! Hey there, Ely, boy!" several of the militiamen were shouting outside the jail, their voices brimming with the surprise they had carried back from the war. "You in there?"

"Here I am," Ely replied, pressing his face against the window of the cell. Since moving into the jail he had spent so many hours staring through that hole while the giant rolled on the floor and Rain Hawk flitted on her mysterious errands that he now saw the grid of wooden bars even with his eyes closed. "I got ears to hear with. What you want with me?"

The soldiers lounging outside the jail all began talking at once, each one eager to deliver the news, but they finally yielded to the powerful voice of the blacksmith, Asher Gurley: "Ely, we found him, right up there at Sandusky!"

"Found who?" said Ely, edgy from lack of sleep, already feeling along his spine the same tingle of foreboding he had felt when approaching that stump out front of the spice girl's hut.

"Why, your brother Ezra!" Gurley boomed.

"My *brother?* Where—how—how'd you turn him up?"

"One night," said Gurley, "we got to talking with a company from Kentucky, swapping family names, you know how you do. One name led to another, and before we knew it, this mean-looking scout—great red beard on him, scars all over his face, one ear tore off—spoke up fiercelike and said, 'I'm Ezra Jackson. Who wants to know?' 'You got a redheaded brother named Ely?' we said. 'Did,' he said. 'You all used to live down around near Louisville?' 'Did,' he said, more sunk down. You ought to seen the look on him when we told him you was here in Roma!"

Christ Jesus, after all these years of hunting—his brother found. Ely clung to the bars of the window, feeling weak, confused between hope and fear. A great cry was tearing at him, but he would not let it out. With his face set hard, he said, "What's he—what's he like?"

The militiamen shuffled awkwardly in the street, heavy-muscled brawlers and boasters, suddenly tongue-tied. They all looked at Gurley, who finally said, "Well, he ain't pretty." Three or four of the soldiers guffawed, uneasy. "Truth to tell, he's fair beat up. Limps bad, one eye don't look square at you, and there's a few chunks of his scalp missing. From what he said, he's been fighting Indians five years, and he looks like he's come out on the short end a few times."

Did he say why he abandoned me? Ely wanted to ask, remembering Ezra's last words: *I love you, Ely boy. Don't you ever doubt it. Ain't we brothers? I'll come back and fetch you just as soon as I get me a job and a place to live.* But Ely said only: "Where's he at now?"

"We tried to get him to come along home with us," Gurley explained, "but he signed on for another month at the war. Said he wanted to stick with General Harrison and put lead in as many Indians as he could before the fighting stopped. The other Roma boys, the sharpshooters, they'll bring him back with them in October." Gurley's face broke into a gap-toothed grin. "Ain't that something? Ain't that just the cat's meow? Finding your brother after all these years of looking!"

The militiamen all grinned at him, expecting a shout, a hat flung in the air, some show of celebration. "It sure is," Ely said quietly, "it surely is."

Disappointed, the soldiers tramped off down the

street. Ely backed away from the window and slumped onto the pallet where the giant lay. The big man stirred, gave a grunt. In the half-light Ely patted him on the haunch, whispering, "My brother, my own brother," although there was no one to understand his words. Rain Hawk was out on one of her errands—off gathering weeds, he figured, or praying to one of her forest gods—and so he had to keep his bewildering hurt bottled up inside, unshared. He felt torn up, loving his brother, hungry to see him, yet at the same time afraid, thinking, if Ezra got killed in the fields of Canada, I wouldn't have to face him, wouldn't have to find words for all these years of abandonment and yearning.

Quietly the office door opened and footsteps approached over the carpet, so quietly that Owen looked up from his desk only when Mademoiselle Rozier's strangely accented voice—an amalgam of French and Shawnee and frontier English—said to him, "I come to tell you the story of the rabbit's death."

Even before glimpsing her distraught face, framed between twin plaits of jet-black hair, Owen realized from her voice alone that she had worked herself into a state of extreme agitation. "Please sit down," he urged, drawing up one of the Windsor chairs he had brought with him from Philadelphia. She sat facing him, perched on the edge of the seat as if ready to leap up and run away. She wore the British officer's coat of lobster red, decorated with silver brooches and beads. "Might I bring you some tea?" he offered.

"No, I want to speak. I am waiting for the words."
Her eyes closed and she rocked on the chair edge.
Suddenly, without looking at him, she began speaking
as if in trance: "When I saw them in my clearing, the
rabbit and the bearman, I thought they were a vision.
It was the evening, and the earth was dim. I had been
fasting, to lure the spirit-helpers. If Our Grandmother
sent me a vision, I hoped my people would let me
return home. The woods were silent, as in dream, and
the winds slept. The sky makes a circle around the
woods, and the woods make a circle around my hut,
and the walls of my hut make a circle around my fire.
There I stood at the center of the circles, praying, and
then I saw these two spirits, the big and the little,
coming toward me. My mother had told me about
such spirits—the rabbitmen who live under the ground
and possess secrets of power, the ancient bearmen who
live in caves, keepers of the old ways. So I was not
surprised to see the two of them in my clearing."

She paused, threshing among memories with a look
of anguish on her face. Owen knew instinctively that
he must not interrupt her, lest he break the trance.
In a moment she resumed: "They walked until they
covered my doorway. Did I want to see the big one
do tricks? the little one said. The name he called him
was Pennsylvania ironman, but I knew it was the
bearman, and I was not afraid of him. 'I do not want
tricks,' I told him, 'I want power.' 'The big one will
crush you,' he said, 'and pull you apart until you
crack.' 'I know this bearman,' I said, 'and he will not
hurt me.' And to the big one I made the sign of wel-

come. 'Do not show me your tricks,' I said, 'give me power.' "

The girl trembled on the edge of her chair, buffeted by memory, yet her voice was like the steady drone of a dulcimer: "The pack the bearman carried was full of medicine, the rabbit said. Medicine strong enough to bring the dead back to life, he said, strong enough to drive the white men across the Ohio River and fill the woods with game. He would sell me a bundle of this medicine for much money. 'I have no money,' I told him. 'Then dance for me, and that will be payment,' he said. This I did, for the sake of the medicine bundle. He came inside the hut with me and lit the lantern and watched me dance as though I were a horse for sale. Still I believed he was a spirit."

Breaking her story, she leaned forward, eyes closed, braids swinging. Because she seemed to have exhausted her store of words, Owen risked giving a gentle nudge: "I know this is painful—"

Immediately the entranced voice resumed: "When I grew tired I said to him, 'Now give me the medicine.' But the rabbit pinched me and said I must dance. 'Stupid witch,' he called me. 'Wild pig of the woods,' he called me. 'The medicine,' I said, and when I stopped the dance he jabbed me with a burning stick from the fire. I cried out, and he laughed. Then I knew he was no spirit, but a man, an evil man, and I cursed him. It was dark and terrible in my heart, for the trick he had played me, and I screamed at him every one of my mother's curses. He chased me around the hut with his burning stick, jabbing me, laughing, until I ran outside. There the bèarman caught him by the scruff of his neck. The big one lifted him up and looked at me, and I nodded, yes, yes. And the bearman carried him to the hominy stump and pounded the rabbit into the hole—three times, four times, until the screaming stopped."

"Then the giant ran away?" Owen asked, forced to speak.

She rocked back in her chair, relaxing, the worst of the story behind her. "I fell down on the ground and lay there. I had not eaten for three days, and my body fell and slept. In the night, when the moon shone, the big one's moaning woke me, and I saw him beside the stump, holding the rabbit's legs. I called to him, and he carried me into my hut, and covered me, and signed to me his name: Bear Walks. He asked me where his people were buried, but I did not know his people. So I told him of the cave at Door-in-Rock, where there are bones of the ancient ones. Then he left me, and I knew nothing until the sun shone. I wanted to bury the rabbit, to hide him, but I could not pull him from the stump. And that is when Tree-Who-Sings found me."

"Tree-Who-Sings?" said Owen.

"It is what the bearman calls Ely Jackson." Tears seeped from beneath her closed eyes. "That is the story of the rabbit's death. You see, I killed him. You must let the bearman go."

In order to still the trembling in his hands, Owen grasped the quill and began writing. Immediately the nib split, blotching the paper with ink. All his lawyerly training unraveled and he was left speechless, watching this girl weep under the weight of memory. She cried silently, her tears seeping like water around the leather seal of a pump.

"Perhaps I—" he began, but his voice caught.

"I will tell this in court," she said, her eyes blinking open, her body drawing erect in the chair again, "and they will set Bear Walks free." In a moment she had thrown off the load of misery and sat across the desk from him as bold and defiant as she must have seemed to the dwarf.

Owen's heart was too sluggish to follow this girl's moods. He felt rudimentary next to her, primitive. "Before he saved you by killing the dwarf, the giant helped him intimidate and assault other women. A jury is not likely to forgive that."

"I do not believe he would hurt anyone," she declared.

"He made a convincing threat, and that was enough."

"And for this they will hang him? Because he scares people? Because he has black hair like me and the face of an Indian? Because he cannot speak your words and say what is in his heart?"

"I can't predict what a jury will decide."

The green eyes snapped furiously. "You want him to hang, to be rid of him!"

"I want to uphold the law," Owen replied irritably, the thirty days of trail still aching in his bones.

"Kill! Kill! Kill!" she cried, her eyes blazing like a madwoman's. "It is all you know!"

When Owen rose from the desk to calm her, she

leaped backward as if snakebitten, bumped against the unlatched door, and fled into the street.

He watched her go in a rage of helplessness. The skirts whipped about her ankles and the red soldier's coat flared out behind from her wild running. Even if I do get her to testify, he thought, no one will believe her. In the town's mind, she was a half-breed sorceress. But Owen believed her, knowing he would dream about that lamplit dance, those curses, those wounded eyes.

While he leaned in the doorway of his office, rehearsing courtroom speeches with a sense of futility, dusk settled onto Roma. It's not true, he assured himself: I don't want him hanged. All I want is justice, the rule of law.

Voices bragged and whispered in the street, some emerging from the vicinity of lanterns, others from the darkness. Across the square the wavering shadows of men were tugging boards from windows. The wood released its nails with an animal screech.

Outside the jail a crowd had gathered, murmuring words that Owen could not make out. He did recognize in their voices the tone of dread, the hushed murderous expectancy that had crept over the town while the men were away at war, and which the giant's coming had intensified. Useless to go over there. They would only grumble at him for bringing this monster home alive, as they were doubtless griping at Ely now through the lattice window. Several men were crouched next to the opening, peering in at the dark shapes in the cell, measuring the huge shadow against their imaginings of giants.

From the blacksmith shop the clang of Asher Gurley's hammer boomed through the dusk. Those would be the new hinges, Owen guessed, hinges for the jail cell strong enough to withstand the might of that outrageous prisoner. Clang on clang, the smith hammered muscle into the iron, and the whole town seemed to be listening, intent upon the caging of the beast.

Owen tried to imagine himself shut up in that cell, as Ely was, with such an unpredictable creature. In the past week Ely had not even been able to go outside for a stretch, since each time he had left the jail the bearman had burst out after him. So there Ely sat, as much a prisoner as the giant was, unable to forget for a minute that some stupid animal loyalty to him had lured the giant back to this wretched end.

A voice overhead called down: "Mr. Lightfoot, your supper is ready."

The lawyer tilted his face upward to smile at Mrs. Forbes, whose bonnet-framed face was thrust from the upstairs window. "Yes, my dear, I'm on my way."

Turning to go in, still musing about Ely and the giant, Owen noticed that a fearful silence had spread through the street. No more animal howls from the walls of cabins as nails were drawn, no more banging of the blacksmith's hammer, no more shuffling from the crowd of men who still lurked about the jail's window. The town seemed ready to scream, with a single shuddering cry that would loose its pent-up terror like gushing steam.

The silence grew so oppressive that Owen found himself yearning for any small noise. What suddenly came was the brutal clang of iron on iron again, this time from the jail, a furious metal hammering that seemed to beat inside his chest. For a moment he thought, Good God, he's murdering Ely. But then as the strokes rang on and on, he knew it was the blacksmith nailing the hinges into place, hammering spikes deep enough into the logs to cage an earthquake.

15

"I AIN'T HIS KEEPER," ELY RANTED ONE NIGHT
soon after the new hinges had been installed. "If
he breaks free, that's their lookout. Why in blazes
should I lie here waiting for the trial, while any day
my brother might come riding into town?"

In the half-light of the cell, Rain Hawk usually let
his tirades wash over her without answering. This time
she said, "You go sleep at the lawyer's place. In here
you will go crazy."

"And leave you by yourself with Bear Walks?"

"I will go with you," she said. "The sight of him
also makes me hurt."

And so the two of them unrolled their blankets on
the lawyer's carpet. Ely could not say whether he loved
or hated her. No word of affection had passed between them. She had nursed him through fever, but
with cool skill, as she might have nursed a bird with
a broken wing.

At night as they lay side by side in the tense darkness, he whispered, "I wish to heaven I'd taken your

caution when you left that smashed rabbit on the lawyer's stairway. You did mean it for a caution, didn't you?"

"I did. But you ran after him like a wolf on a scent."

"I wanted to see who belonged to those feet, those great big feet. That's all I wanted. Not this . . ." His voice trailed off.

Later, when the giant's thrashing shattered the stillness, Ely covered his ears with the blanket and pretended not to hear.

Rain Hawk said, "He will not stay in their box."

Four times in the following weeks, the giant broke from jail. First he smashed the wooden grating at the window, then he tore out the metal one that replaced it. Next he walked through the open door when Mrs. Jenkins unlocked it to fetch his dinner pan. And finally he walked through the door when it was closed, bursting hinges, braces, and iron lock.

Except for the afternoon when Mrs. Jenkins went to collect the dinner dish, each time he broke out at night, shocking the village with sounds of splintered wood and tortured metal. No one within earshot, least of all Sheriff Jenkins, was anxious to chase him in the dark. Those wakened by the noise shoved cupboards against their doors and waited for daylight. Before morning the giant could have murdered them one by one, or could have walked unmolested into the next county. Instead, like an escaped bull, he snuffled around town, rubbing against water troughs and hitching posts, casting huge shadows onto windows, scrabbling against shut doors, sniffing about until morning.

At daybreak, cabin doors would open a crack and eyes would peer out to behold the giant stretched on the ground in front of the lawyer's office, snoring prodigiously. Even though no one had been murdered in the night, no horses torn apart, no doors kicked in, still the giant lying sprawled there in the dirt seemed to the villagers like a dozing earthquake, a rockslide about to let go. Guns thrust from windows, yet nobody ventured into the street on those jailbreak mornings until Ely—wearing a blanket around his shoulders against the October chill—emerged from the lawyer's office to roust the giant from sleep. "Up, big fella," he coaxed. "Come on, back to the jailhouse with you. How'd you bust out this time?" Instead of crushing Ely, the great man rolled ponderously over and rose to his feet, kept on rising to that absurd inhuman stature, then tagged after him for all the world like a trained ox.

On the afternoon when Mrs. Jenkins opened the cell door, leveling a pistol at him, the giant simply walked past her, ignoring the wild shot that she fired into the wall. He ambled into the sunlight, hair caked with dirt and sawdust, beard matted with food, lips cracked, yellow eyes wincing at the glare. People surrounded him with pitchforks and axes and guns, trying to herd him back toward the jail.

Mrs. Jenkins rushed outside, struggling to reload the pistol and yelling, "Kill him! Kill him!"

Others echoed her: "Shoot him! Shoot him! Kill him now!"

Mrs. Jenkins flung down the pistol, seized a pitchfork, and jabbed it blindly into the giant's arm. The big man bellowed, amazing the villagers, who had never thought he possessed such a voice. He looked around bewildered, then snatched the fork by its tines and cracked Mrs. Jenkins over the head with the handle.

The onlookers drew back, rifles and axes lifted. They would have shot him right then, while he lumbered about inside the circle, if Ely had not come running up the street, shouting, "Leave him be! Leave him be! He ain't been tried yet!"

"He went for Mrs. Jenkins here," said Jonas Spinks, who had come limping from the stable with a bull-whip. The woman sat in the dirt, clutching her temples and sobbing.

"Well, why'd she go poking at him for?" Ely put his hand on the giant's wounded arm. Flowers of blood spread through the cloth of the sleeve.

The villagers kept shouting for a kill, each one hoping somebody else would fire first. But Ely stood in front of the big man, wheeling from voice to voice, facing them down, taking their hatred upon himself, and at last they lowered their guns.

"Next time he breaks jail we shoot him on sight," warned Spinks. The others nodded, clutching their guns and axes.

But when he next erupted from the jail, five nights later, no one dared chase him into the moonless dark. The stab of the pitchfork seemed to have jarred loose some animal voice in him, for he growled and bellowed through the village until dawn, when he stretched out to sleep on the lawyer's stoop. Although men trained their rifles on him, they did not carry out their threat. It seemed foolish to fire on him there in his mammoth sleep—like pumping lead into a mountain. Besides, people were afraid that if they did not kill him on the first shot they might never get a second. And there seemed too much of him for one shot to kill. So they waited in doorways until Ely, looking more and more sick at heart, arrived to lead the great shambling brute away to jail.

That morning, still nine days before the judge was to arrive for the trial, Mrs. Jenkins dragged the black-smith to the cell. Ely was squatting in the gloom be-side the giant, the two of them eating johnnycakes out of the same bowl.

"You fix it so he stays put in there," she said to Asher Gurley, "or I'll drill a bullet through his thick skull."

The smith gaped at the battered door. The bolt had wrenched free of the lock, and the hinges had twisted like arthritic fingers. "Only thing left to try is chain him," he said.

Ely glowered up at him. "I ain't going to put them on."

Returning with the wrist and ankle irons, the same ones Ely had carried untouched in his saddlebags on the hunt, the smith shoved them into the cell and said, "You got to do it, son."

Ely stared at the chains. "I ain't sunk that low."

"If you don't he'll never live to see the judge." The smith stood in the broken doorway, not looking at him. "Go on, son."

Sullenly, Ely took up the chains and shackled the

[187]

giant, foot to foot and wrist to wrist, the huge limbs turning in his hands with the unresisting weight of a sleeping child.

Gurley looped a chain around one of the logs in the wall, and this he locked to the giant's ankle irons. "That should hold, unless he pulls this place down." He clapped Ely on the back. "Come on, son, don't let this eat on you. Think of your brother coming. Won't it be grand to see him, after all these years? Quit your stewing. Even if it comes to hanging—well, there's a lot of people have died out here a lot worse ways."

Now the villagers heard the scraping of chains at all hours of day and night, mostly night, when the giant thrashed about in his cell. Everyone within earshot abandoned hope of peace and quiet. Owen could hear the chains from his desk, where the pages of legal argument were gathering like paper cliffs of futility, and from his table, where he spoke soothingly with Mrs. Forbes. Ely could hear the clanking everywhere, even in his rare sleep on the lawyer's floor. Rain Hawk listened to the rattling of chains from the shadows outside the window of the jail, where she kept watch on the bearman and sang medicine songs, her hands busy weaving baskets from strips of split oak.

But most of all Mrs. Jenkins heard his thrashing from her bedroom above the cell. To quiet him, she set about starving him. After three days without food, the giant was dragging about his cell like a ghost, his voice rasped away, staggering under the weight of the chains.

Each morning Ely curled into a tighter ball on the lawyer's carpet, paralyzed by inner voices, unwilling to face the giant. He tried thinking about his brother —the upcoming visit, the grief to unload, the words that must be found. How would Ezra the Indian-killer feel about Rain Hawk? Maybe him and me can clear some land, farm a little, thought Ely. But he could not imagine moving back to the cabin on Bone Creek, out near the spot where he had discovered the huge boot-prints. He could not move into Roma, either, for he had no work here, and the folks seemed to him tainted by hatred. Moving back east would mean even more people to bump into. That only left the west. Maybe one night he should just spring the giant free and lead him out there, into the unpeopled territory. Would Rain Hawk and Ezra go along? And would Bear Walks shadow him like a brother forever?

Meanwhile, the giant was dying, and the only ones who knew, besides Mrs. Jenkins, were Rain Hawk, who could see him dragging weakly about in the cell, and the children, who stopped on their errands to peer at him through the window. When the children told of their discovery at home—"He's terrible sick, cain't hardly stand up"—mothers and fathers pretended not to hear. They slept soundly again, since the prisoner had lost his voice.

Two nights before the judge was to arrive, the giant seemed to recover some of his strength, for he kept the whole town awake with his thrashing and bellow-ing. In the morning Mrs. Jenkins noticed on the floor beside him a new oak basket. Seeing her at the door, he leaped against his chains. On the following night the spice girl managed again to slip a basket of food to him through the window.

By the eve of the judge's visit, the giant was creating such an uproar that men decided to camp around the jail with torches and guns, fearing he might buckle the wall or snap his irons. The watchers had trouble staying awake because they had spent that day on a township hunt. The judge's visit, with its promise of deliverance from this caged beast, had put it into their heads to clear the township of the uncaged ones. While the men had been away at the war, wolves had been devouring their chickens, panthers had strewn meadows with half-eaten sheep, rattlesnakes had felled children, bears had frightened horses into running wild and cows into drying up. Every morning women had returned from the bloody pastures with eyes more haunted. Back now from the war, the men would not put up with this slaughter.

So on the day preceding the judge's visit, hunters scattered before dawn around the borders of the township. Women and children and livestock were shut up inside cabins. At the sounding of a horn, which made a circuit of the township from trumpeter to trumpeter, the men on the boundaries marched forward, beating the bushes, driving animals before them with the remorselessness of a brushfire. When the ring tightened to half a mile in diameter, churning with prey, another horn sounded, and the hunters began to shoot. The circle drew tighter; they fired again, again, and only quit shooting when no more life quivered within their ring. Then they reckoned the kill: 103 deer, 21 bears, 13 wolves, 7 foxes, 3 panthers, uncounted turkeys and uncountable smaller game, such as possums and rabbits and raccoons. The meat was divvied up among the shooters, all except the piddling scrawny game, which was left for the dogs.

So those who stood watch around the jail that night were tired from the day's hunt. Their wives were home skinning deer, their daughters plucking turkeys. Their dogs were in the woods gnawing on the carcasses of squirrels. The men themselves stood about in the glare of torches listening to the monster heave against his chains. Each time he charged, the logs of the jail resounded. Tomorrow the judge would come to begin the trial, and the men felt that the very presence of the law in Roma, with its robes and curly wigs, would license them to hang the giant.

16

THE JUDGE WAS DELIVERED INTO ROMA IN A FOUR-horse wagon, where he sat enthroned beneath an awning on an upholstered armchair, smiling at the crowd with the high-and-mighty bearing of a lord posing for a portrait. He was new to the circuit, so the villagers examined him carefully. He was quite old and frail, and his face was pinched tight as if he had been staring for years into a strong wind. He was dressed so grandly, from high-heeled boots through swallowtailed coat to chalky wig, that the townspeople were a little surprised to see him climb down from his upholstered chair into the dirt of Roma.

"Would someone be so kind as to direct me to Mr. Lightfoot?" he asked in a quavering voice.

Children ran to fetch the lawyer. The adults kept staring at this bewigged old man. Had he posed as anything but a judge, they would have despised him. Clearly he was unfit to ride a horse or chop a tree or milk a cow. Set down by himself in the woods, without stores or servants, he would not last a week. But his lordly manner and costume suited their notion of the grandeur appropriate to the law. Even Owen Lightfoot, who came hurrying up to meet him, was no dandy to rival this Moses Pond.

The two men retired to the lawyer's office, conferring in their learned language. They were followed by the driver of the wagon, a sag-bellied and sad-eyed man of about thirty named Fidelio Kingsbury, who turned out to be the prosecuting attorney. He carried the judge's upholstered chair on his shoulder and cast over the heads of the crowd a look of intense boredom.

As soon as the three men were closeted in the office, Judge Pond lowered himself into the armchair, shut his eyes, and began reciting procedures for the trial in the manner of a schoolmaster repeating sums. "Of course," he said by way of conclusion, "if you were to put up only a token defense, Mr. Lightfoot—"

"Your Honor?" said Owen, taken aback.

The old dandy gave him an indulgent smile. "Anyone foolish enough to defend such an unpopular client should at least have the good sense to make that defense a feeble one. The sooner this business is accomplished, the less damage you will suffer."

"But, Your Honor, the law—"

"Yes, yes, the law. And what of those ambitions you confided to me during our lunch in Columbus, Mr. Lightfoot? Have you abandoned them entirely? How do you suppose one becomes a judge? Eh? Not by defending scoundrels and unpopular causes."

"Are you suggesting I rig the trial?"

The judge raised his hands in mock horror. "Nothing of the sort, my dear sir, nothing of the sort. I merely thought you might wish to discharge the case as painlessly as possible."

Hearing his own craven thoughts uttered by the judge himself, Owen fell back on his dignity, saying, "I intend to provide my client with the full protection of the law."

"As you wish, Mr. Lightfoot. There's no harm in making a friendly inquiry, is there?" Aided by the prosecutor, who had maintained a bored silence throughout the discussion, the judge unbent his spindly legs. "Don't mistake me, young man. I was merely trying to keep you from ruining your career."

"I am quite capable of looking after myself," Owen said.

The indulgent smile wavered on the judge's lips. "Very well. Suit yourself. I shall see you in court three days hence." In the midst of his shuffling exit, followed by the prosecutor bearing the armchair, the judge turned around. "You are in for a bitter lesson, Mr. Lightfoot, if you imagine this place to be even remotely like Philadelphia."

The next three days were spent by Judge Pond politicking among the villagers, and by Fidelio Kingsbury preparing his case. Anyone who had so much as glimpsed the giant's bootprints came forward to volunteer information, which the prosecutor recorded in a ledger. His air of disdain inspired the witnesses to embellish the giant's brief transit with all the horrors and grudges they could recall from their years in the Ohio country.

Owen spent much of the time fretting about his future. He would soon be thirty-two, the age of Meriwether Lewis on his return from the Pacific. And what had he accomplished? His dream of becoming an explorer had been dissolved by the acid reality of the wilderness. The only woman for whom he had ever deeply cared was locked in the room upstairs, pale with fear that he would abandon her again. The small legacy of idealism and money inherited from his Quaker parents was nearly exhausted. And still he was nothing but a backwoods lawyer. Now even that flimsy identity might be torn from him. What did that leave?

The more people crowded into Roma for the trial, hungry for a hanging, swapping rumors about the giant, the less stomach Ely had for humanity. It angered him the way folks lined up to spin their murderous yarns for the prosecutor, the way they fawned over that wheedling, rickety old peacock of a judge.

But on the day appointed for the trial, it was Ely who led the giant through a gantlet of faces to the newly whitewashed courthouse. Glancing along the ranks of spectators, Ely wondered if one of those faces was his brother's, scarred and stained, broken like the others by a mocking smile. Rain Hawk, decked out in all her bangles, slipped through the crowd behind him, leaving a trail of gossip, insults, and frowns burning in her wake.

People had been arriving for two days, walking or riding in from the backwoods, drawn here to see this freak of nature whom tinkers and scouts had described on their rounds. The courtroom was packed so tightly that deputies had trouble clearing a path for the prisoner to slouch through. When he squeezed past, fully eight feet tall and heavy in proportion, dressed in skins and with a shaggy black mane surrounding his head like a thunder cloud, the onlookers who had journeyed from miles away felt the spectacle more than made up for their wearisome travels.

Judge Pond, resplendent in cloud-white wig, black robe, and ruffled shirt, sat in his luxurious armchair at a table in the front. The giant rested on a stonecutter's bench, with Ely alongside to keep him docile. After studying the defendant for a moment, Judge Pond raised his white eyebrows and pursed his lips, as if to whistle. The crowd kept up a buzz of amazement.

Owen rose to speak. "Your Honor, I move that there be a change of venue to Cleveland or Columbus, for my client cannot receive a fair trial in Roma."

The judge surveyed the audience. They were edgy, explosive, crammed so tightly in the room that sounds could have passed among them from bone to bone. He knew how swiftly such a crowd could spark into a mob. Controlling them would require every bit of his rhetorical skill, as well as minimal cooperation from this headstrong attorney. At length he announced, "I see no reason to doubt the fairness or judgment of this community, Mr. Lightfoot."

The jury was impaneled, and the charge was read: Bear Walks, the defendant, of mixed blood, had, on the 10th of August, 1813, on Cairo Trace three miles east of Roma, Ohio, in the County of Pilgrim, murdered his employer, one Epaphrus Matthews, peddler . . .

The spectators strained to follow this legal rigmarole. The giant appeared not to listen at all, but only gazed out over the jammed courtroom with sleepy eyes. He seemed indifferent to the entire business, not even paying attention when the dwarf's bloody suit, the rucksack aromatic with spices, and the wad of paper money were entered as evidence.

Did any memory of killing the dwarf still glimmer like a firefly inside his thick skull? Owen wondered.

In a voice that was at once aggrieved and haughty, Kingsbury summarized his case. Defendant had been hired by the victim in Pittsburgh, had journeyed with him from door to door, terrorizing and helping to rob lone women. This practice continued along the entire route from Pittsburgh to Roma, until, on the night of August 10, the pair of brigands had a falling out near where Bone Creek traverses the Cairo Road, and there the defendant concluded the argument by jamming Matthews into a hominy stump.

Throughout the prosecutor's speech, which was embroidered with remarks calculated to flatter the jury, Owen kept rising to voice objections, and the judge kept overruling him, growing more brusque with each interruption. The case means nothing to Kingsbury, thought Owen. He's not seeking justice, with his smirks and verbal flourishes; he's running for office, before the biggest audience that could have been assembled in Roma.

Finally exasperated beyond bearing, Owen cried, "Your Honor, this is a court of law, not a political rally!"

"If you make one more frivolous outburst, Mr.

Lightfoot," warned the judge, "I shall be forced to hold you in contempt."

Meanwhile, the big man over whom these quarrels were raging blinked lazily. His eyes reminded onlookers of the indifference of snowstorms and fevers and floods. They felt invisible before his muddy yellow stare. Ely Jackson sat next to him with head adroop, shoulders slumped, gaze on the floor.

The jury followed the proceedings from deacon's benches, faces grave, hands searching for places to rest on knees or inside pockets. All twelve of them were well known to Owen. They had helped settle this territory, had fought, many of them, in the Revolution and Indian wars, had served in the militia, had lost wives or children to the hazards of Ohio. Amid the scuffing of feet, the coughing, the legal sparring, these twelve weathered men studied the giant with sidelong glances. Even when they looked away from him, they could feel his wild presence.

At length the prosecutor was finished, and Owen, gripped by a sense of despair, rose to offer his rebuttal. "You see here before you an idiot, a childlike man ignorant of speech. Despite his appearance, he is not a bloodthirsty beast. He traveled with Ely Jackson and myself in utter peacefulness for days on end. It is true that he killed Mr. Matthews, but I will show that he did so in order to prevent the scoundrel from torturing —and quite possibly killing—Mademoiselle Marie Antoinette Rozier."

The courtroom sizzled with whispers. People stood on tiptoes to get a look at where the girl sat on the front bench, decked out in her beads and shells.

The judge rapped his mallet on the table. After the crowd simmered down, he ordered the prosecutor to call witnesses.

Kingsbury complained to the jury, "Mr. Owen would have us believe that the defendant cannot speak English. Yet the very children tell of conversing with him through his prison window."

"Yes!" several children shouted. "He surely can talk!"

Parents hushed them and the judge hammered.

"He can growl bear talk at least!" a man shouted.

The audience roared. Judge Pond grew red in the face from pounding the table. "Silence! Silence!" He gazed nearsightedly into the air above their heads, and when quiet had been restored, he declared, "Very well, then, let us proceed with testimony."

Responding to the prosecutor's questions, Habakuk Bennett told about seeing the dwarf in Pittsburgh bargaining for a foundryman to carry his rucksack. Three women testified about having been robbed by the peddler. "He told me this ironman was the most vicious creature ever to walk the earth," one of them said, "who'd kill me in a minute on his say-so and drink every last drop of my blood." Next, Jared Scranton, who raised hogs on Cairo Trace, spoke of watching the little man and the huge one pass his clearing headed toward Roma on the day of the murder. Ely was asked to recount his discovery of the corpse and the bootprints, and this he did, mumbling his words. Finally Mrs. Jenkins testified about the giant's jailbreaks, concluding, "If there's any stronger beast alive, I don't want to meet him."

Heads bobbed as she spoke. The villagers could

recall only too well the sound of his bellowing, the tremors in their cabin walls as he scratched his shoulders against their eaves, the sight of him stretched in the dirt like a drowsing catastrophe.

Although Owen in turn questioned each witness sharply, every answer bound the giant more firmly to the peddler's crimes. The only mitigating words came from Ely, who had been dreading this hour. It was bad enough to have hunted the giant down, lured him to Roma, and kept him chained in jail; now he had to speak of these deeds in public. In a scratchy voice that no one could hear beyond the first few rows, Ely told of the cave, the gifts, the return; he told of feeling a stronger and stronger bond toward the big man, of being nursed through fever, of sleeping next to him. "It's like we're brothers," he murmured, and this set off a round of snickering in the courtroom. By the end of the confession his voice had dwindled to a whisper. At no point could he bring himself to look into those impassive yellow eyes.

There were more questions Owen had in mind to ask, but he was unwilling to put his partner through any more suffering. So at last he called Mademoiselle Rozier to the stand, and again the room crackled with gossip.

She had done her best to masquerade as a white girl for the trial, wearing a dress of sky-blue cloth instead of deerskins, and her black hair in a bun instead of braids. But the hem of the dress was tricked out with ribbons, her moccasins were ornately beaded, and the necklaces clacked as she took her seat in the witness stand. No white girl could have gazed so un-flinchingly at the spectators. Owen feared he would have to coax her along through her testimony, but no sooner had he asked her the first question than she began reciting, practically word for word, the entire story she had told him in his office, without any show of emotion, as if it were a tale handed down through generations.

"When I saw them in my clearing, the rabbitman and bearman, I thought they were a vision. It was evening, and the earth was dim . . ." The crowd grew quiet in order to catch the singsong of her words, overhearing the witchy phrases—spirit helpers, se-crets of power—as if eavesdropping on the devil. She told how the dwarf had promised her great medicine if she would dance, and how she had danced, danced until she would drop, and still he drove her on, burned her arms with a stick from the fire, told how, when she ran outside cursing, the giant seized the dwarf, pounded him into the stump, and then moaned all night beside the sack of bones. "You see," she fin-ished in the stunned silence, "I am the one who killed the rabbit. You must let the bearman go."

Owen was surprised to find the jurors gazing thoughtfully at her, as if they might succumb to the spell of her words.

Immediately the prosecutor set out to break the charm in his cross-examination. "You are a woman of Indian blood, are you not, Miss Rozier?"

"Shawnee blood," she answered. "Shawnee and French."

"Shawnee? A tribe with whom we are presently at war? And what species of Indian would you guess the defendant to be?"

She gazed long at the giant. "I do not know."

"Mongrel Indian, perhaps? And how do you earn your living?"

"I make tea and baskets. I sell spices."

"Is that your only source of income?" Kingsbury persisted.

Owen leaped to his feet. "Mademoiselle Rozier's race and means of livelihood have no relevance to the case, Your Honor."

"It has all the relevance in the world, Your Honor," said Kingsbury, "if Miss Rozier makes a practice of thievery."

The crowd babbled; the lawyers stood nose-to-nose, glaring; the judge cried for order. Order was slow in returning, and fragile. The girl betrayed no emotion, not the least anger or shame, and that in itself was proof of her alien nature.

"Did you not suspect," Kingsbury resumed, "that Mr. Matthews, being an itinerant salesman, might carry money on his person? And when Mr. Jackson discovered you trying to pull the victim from the stump, were you not searching for that money? Did you not in fact incite the defendant—a creature of your own blood—to commit the murder?"

"This is outrageous!" Owen shouted, all courtroom etiquette flung aside. "Mademoiselle Rozier is not on trial!"

Kingsbury matched him in volume, bellowing, "Isn't

the giant in fact your monstrous puppet, and aren't you a witch?"

No one paid much attention to the crossfire of insults that broke out between the lawyers or to the judge's ineffectual cries, for in the midst of it the giant surged to his feet, overturning his bench and tumbling Ely to the floor. Maybe he was weary of the proceedings, or confused, or sleepy; whatever his reasons, he simply left, towering above those who scattered from him in all directions, stepping heavily over members of the jury who had tipped the deacon's bench in their panic, ignoring the judge who hammered madly for order. Ely just managed to grab one of his arms, and clinging to it was dragged into the street.

Without paying any heed to Ely and without glancing at the men who crowded after him, the giant tramped back to the jail and lay down on his cornshuck mattress.

"He don't mean no harm!" Ely hollered at the mob outside the window. "He couldn't catch the drift of that trial, is all!" When they yelled for him to clap on the irons and chain the brute to the jailhouse wall, he protested, "There's no call for that. He won't stir again, now he's back in here."

If Ely didn't chain him, they swore they'd shoot the beast right then and there. Rifles bristled in the doorway and between the twisted bars of the window. The giant lay studying them with indifferent eyes. If he gets up to see who's pestering him and spoiling his rest, we're both dead, thought Ely. And for an instant he wanted the hunt to end that way—Bear Walks rising, guns booming, the two of them dying together. But the coppery taste of death in his mouth frightened him. And so he took up the irons and shackled them onto the unresisting man.

Presently Owen excused his way through the crowd at the door, his bow tie dangling askew, his shirt soaked with sweat. "You all get away now," he pleaded, shooing the mob from the hallway and window. "Can't you see he's chained up?"

The men retreated, but only far enough to build a ring of fires around the jail, where they would keep vigil through the night with rifles across their knees.

"He's done it now," said Owen, sagging to the dirt beside Ely. "Defendants don't just walk out in the middle of their trial. If only you could have governed him—"

"You're welcome to try your hand at it." Ely took from his shirt pouch a horn spoon and began digging viciously at the dirt.

"I'm not blaming you," said Owen. "But now he has frightened them all out of their wits, including the judge."

"What did old white wig do?"

"He adjourned the trial until tomorrow morning."

"Is Kingsbury going to have another go at Rain Hawk? Once or twice, I like to jumped up and strangled him."

"No, I'm sure he feels he's done enough to discredit her testimony. All that remains is for each of us to present summary arguments, and then the jury will deliberate." Overcome by weariness, Owen found himself leaning against the giant, and he realized that he feared the great man less, the more the townspeople reviled him. "But I'm afraid the jury has already decided. You can read it in their faces, as clear as labels on bottles. The whole business is a mockery."

Ely kept gouging the dirt. "What did you expect?"

"Justice . . . the law . . ." Owen began. Then he shrugged, all passion wrung out of him. He tried to recollect the zeal he had felt on that first morning of the hunt, when he had set out with Ely to defend the community against lawlessness. "You did your part," he said at last, "getting him here and keeping him in jail. My part was seeing justice done, and I failed."

"You didn't have much say over that. There's too much hate in the air. Hate and fear thicker than woodsmoke."

The giant rolled over on his mattress, the chains rasping and cornshucks crackling. Outside, fires burned in a ring about the jail, and around each fire sat a ring of watchful men. What difference did the woman's testimony make, the men were saying, when she was a half-breed? And as for Ely Jackson, hadn't he called himself brother to that monster?

17

THE ROMA SHARPSHOOTERS RETURNED IN THE night from Canada, bringing word that our troops had routed the British and cut Tecumseh and his braves to pieces at a battle on the River Thames. Those who kept watch outside the jail fed more wood to their bonfires and shot off their guns in celebration.

Wakened by the shots, alone in his cell with the giant, Ely turned this news over in his mind. That would break the Indians' back, he knew, this killing of Tecumseh, their untouchable hero. Rain Hawk would have wailed to hear it. But she was away gathering stuff for the giant's funeral—elm bark, clay paints, sacred tobacco. For the tobacco she would have to ride to the nearest Shawnee villages, on the Auglaize River. "Can't you get some in Roma?" Ely had asked her. "No," she said, "our spirit mothers will not smell the white man's tobacco." "You do mean to come back?" he asked her. She had touched Ely then, a finger on his chest, saying, "I will bury him. After, we can speak."

Outside, one of the watchers asked the returning soldiers, "Where's Ely's brother? Wasn't he supposed to come with you?"

"He was fixing to come," a sharpshooter replied, "but he got too greedy for scalps, wouldn't quit slicing topknots from downed Indians—not just the ones he'd killed, you know, but every one he could find, even the wounded ones. He kept running from body to body and hacking at them with his knife, his whole belt full of hair, his eyes like a crazy man's. Wouldn't quit for anything, until Harrison finally had him taken out and shot."

The words boomed into the cell and slammed Ely flat beneath their smothering weight. Ezra? he thought dazedly. Ezra dead? Shot down like a rabid dog? *I love you, Ely boy. Don't you ever doubt it. Ain't we brothers? I'll come back and fetch you just as soon as I get me a job and a place to live.* Ely caught a few gagging breaths, twisted on the pallet, and then let out a roar of pain.

Cheered by the news from Canada, the watchers in the street kept firing off their guns, so that no one in the village was able to sleep. In the midst of the celebration somebody hurled a rock through Owen's plate glass door. His painted name and the arching gold letters of ATTORNEY exploded with the glass and lay in fragments on his carpet. Owen came downstairs with a lamp and surveyed the shards of gold. A note wrapped around the stone warned: GO ON BACK TO PHILADELPHIA, YOU INDIAN LOVER. Upstairs, Mrs. Forbes sat huddled in a blanket, whimpering for England. Owen surrendered to his fearful thirst and took a sip from the flask of whiskey. Only one sip he told himself—then a second, a third, and then with shaking hands he began packing his books and journals into the trunks he had dragged across the mountains.

At first light, while fathers kept watch outside the jail with bloodshot eyes, children crawled up to the cell window and asked questions of the giant, whose head was thrust against the bars. Where did you come from, Mr. Ironman? What do you eat? Are all your folks giants, or are they people? Have you fought any dragons? Why'd you kill that there midget peddler?

Their chirpy voices whistled about the cell like birdsong, piercing Ely's grief. At the window, daylight flamed around the huge silhouette of the bearman. "He don't understand your talk," Ely said in a kindly way.

He does, the children insisted. You can see it in his eyes. He told us once about a country where everybody else is so monstrous big that he's little-bitty as a child there. He likes us talking with him. Just look at how he grins.

Maybe the chirping voices were right, Ely thought, and the bearman really spoke their lingo. What's he see through those candle-flame eyes? What's he hear inside that bramblebush of a head? There was a placidness in the way the big man stood with his neck yoked through the window, like an ox chewing its cud, ears cocked forward. Best leave him alone with the little ones.

As soon as he turned away from the giant, Ely ached with memories of Ezra. Pappy's Indian-killing blood had doomed him. He could see Ezra dragging Pappy to the grave, carrying Mammy like a broken sack, hugging Caroline and the baby before laying them in the ground. Now Ely hugged himself to stifle his moans. "Ezra!" he cried aloud, the word ripping through him. Now the hunt was over. No brother at the end of it, no confessions, no one to blame or forgive, no face to curse or neck to fling his arms around, a ghost where he needed flesh and bone. He felt like a raft loose on the river, cut free and drifting.

Listening to the bird-voices chattering at the giant —fixing his mind on those sounds, just as he would bite on a bullet to distract himself from the probing of a wound—Ely remembered the children along the way who had leaked out of cabins to swarm after the bearman. He remembered the innkeeper's wife with her floury arms who had refused to say where the giant had gone, remembered Rain Hawk combing fleas from his hair and feeding him with her fingers. None of them had been given blackberries in a seashell by the big man, none had been given a necklace of bear's teeth, none had been nursed by him through fever. Yet they had all been drawn to some animal gentleness in him.

Ely sensed that grace now in the way the giant stretched one shackled hand through the window toward the children, who dropped pebbles into his great paw. The watchers gave a shout and rushed forward to tug the children away from the window.

Bear Walks drew his hand back inside and opened it for Ely to see. Pebbles of milky quartz lay in his palm like the seeds of hills. The giant stuffed them into his shirt pouch, hunkered down and slung a heavy arm across Ely's trembling shoulders.

At nine o'clock, when Owen arrived to conduct them to the courthouse, he found the two of them playing marbles on the dirt floor with the milkwhite pebbles. The agony in his partner's face cut into him. "I heard about your brother, Ely," he said. "I'm sick, just sick at heart. This couldn't have happened at a worse time for you."

"There's never a good time, is there?" Ely fumbled at the big man's shackles. His hands shook so badly that he could not fit the key in the lock.

"I'm afraid you'll have to leave them on," said Owen. "The judge wants him to appear in chains today."

Ely glared out the window at the mocking daylight. There should be no sunshine, only storm clouds and the air full of dust. "In chains? Up front where everybody can see him?"

"The judge is an old man," said Owen, "and he's very shaken."

Ely took him by the shoulders and looked full in his face. "You've gone back to the drink, haven't you?"

"Just a few drops—a taste—" Then Owen told in a rush about his shattered door, the fragments of gold-flaked glass on the carpet, Mrs. Forbes whimpering, the trunks loaded with books.

"So you let them ruin you along with all the rest of it?" said Ely, and then, pitying Owen, he added, "Don't take it on your own shoulders. It ain't your doing."

"Nor yours."

"It's mine if it's anybody's. I could have rode right by that dwarf. I could have lost the bearman's trail. But it just seemed like I couldn't let it alone, couldn't stop once I'd started. I'm bad as my old man and my brother that way, sinking my teeth in something and hanging on like a coon dog."

Owen took a step backward as the giant lurched to his feet. For the first time he missed the spice girl's crooning, her dark movements. "Where is Mademoiselle Rozier?"

"She's rode off collecting things we need to bury him with. He ain't a white man, to get buried our way. So she's going to do him up like the Shawnee do their own. I hope she stays gone until this is over with, else they might roast her for a witch."

"Then what will she do? Where will she go?"

"I have no idea," said Ely.

"Will you stay with her? Look after her?"

Ely grimaced. "You oughtn't to wish me on a dog. She'd do better with my friend here," nodding at the bearded moon face that hovered near the ceiling.

Owen ran his gaze over the giant, from the out-sized gully-leaping boots to the bulging forehead, and thought, He has whirled through our lives like a tornado.

As the partners led their captive from the jail, his iron steps clanking in the street, the men who had watched beside bonfires all night formed a lane of rifles. Children squirmed for a closer look. The giant's passing loosened tongues, and rumors rippled through the crowd, swelling his legend. Ely would not have believed so many people lived within riding distance of Roma, so many woodsmen in skins, women in shawls, children standing tiptoe in moccasins; would not have believed this many bodies could be assembled in Roma even if all the graveyards had been emptied and all the nameless babies dug up from cellars and all the fallen soldiers unmurdered on fields of battle. Walking through this avenue of grim witnesses, Ely fought for breath.

Spectators had kept their places in the courtroom by staying there all night, jammed cheek against kneebone on the floor, and more bodies kept pressing in at the door. The giant's legend had swelled here, also, growing as it passed from ear to ear. Surly with sleeplessness, the throng in the courtroom parted to make way for the two escorts and their prisoner.

The jurymen cast sidelong looks while the giant, guided by prods from Ely, lowered himself onto his bench. Everywhere in the crowd Ely noticed hands twitching, hair straying from bonnets, smudges left unwashed upon the cheeks of children, eyes ringed by fatigue—a hundred signs that a change had been worked in these people overnight. In the jurymen, too, he sensed this change. Their glances slid about the room, not in order to see but to avoid seeing, so that their minds could remain fixed upon the one task before them—to rid themselves of this creature who defied their weapons, their locks, their ceremonies. They had scoured the township clean of wolves and panthers, Englishmen, and Indians. They were not about to falter now in their cleansing.

When the judge doddered in, chalky-pale, fragile, everyone stood up except the giant. The starch had gone out of the old man's ruffles, his wig had grown stringy with sweat, his pinched face had been squeezed tighter. Once enthroned in his armchair, he cast his furtive gaze upon the multitude, but avoided looking at the giant. Few heard his mallet the first time he rapped it on the table, the blow was so feeble. Once the whispering died away, he tried speaking twice before his voice emerged, dry and cracked, to call for Mr. Kingsbury's closing argument.

There could be no shadow of a doubt that the defendant was a murderous villain, the prosecutor began. Whatever his motives for killing the peddler, this creature, this freak of nature, this mindless blackguard had been an accomplice in the foulest deeds of robbery and torture. Should such a brute be set free to walk the roads of Ohio, when the land was already infested with renegades and savages and beasts? The recent good news from the River Thames notwithstanding, the country was still at war, and could not tolerate enemies at home.

The prosecutor's florid speech was punctuated at intervals by the grating of chains, as the giant shifted position on his bench. Everyone else in the courtroom held still, yet it seemed to Ely that no one listened. No one needed to, for Kingsbury was merely echoing the sentiments he had breathed from the air of Roma. Only the giant seemed intent upon the man's voice, cocking his dumb shaggy head to listen as he had listened to the children who sat on the rain barrel outside the jail, his attention caught by the prosecu-

[213]

tor's theatrical gestures. Even when speaking of the giant, Kingsbury did not look at him, nor did the jurors. For all of them he was a presence more felt than seen, like the sun blistering hot on the skin but never looked at squarely with the naked eye. When Kingsbury at length concluded, his arms lifting to sweep the audience in one last gesture of persuasion, he found the giant's eyes fixed on him, and hurriedly sat down.

"Now you, Mr. Lightfoot," the judge said with a quaver. "And kindly avoid provoking the audience or the defendant."

They are provoked already beyond recall, thought Owen as he rose to speak, leaning against the jury box to keep his balance. The hills of paper arguments so carefully piled in his mind were lifted and scattered by the winds of hostility gusting from the audience. He could not think where to begin. Perhaps it was the whiskey as much as the sense of fatalism that led him to speak, not of the trial at all, but of the ships he used to watch on Penn's Landing, sailors in blazing white shirts balanced on the yardarms; of Lewis and Clark's journey to the Pacific; of Peale's menagerie of beasts, the sleek otter and improbable armadillo, the stuffed grizzly bear and buffalo; of reading law in the city of brotherly love, and being seized by a passion for justice.

What the devil's he going on about? Ely wondered. Where's my old cocksure partner? Where's the man who went down the cliff trail looking for the giant? Ely turned away and kept his gaze fixed out the window on the hub of a wagon wheel, in a sign not of disgust but of relinquishment, as if saying to his friend that he knew it was hopeless, had been hopeless from the start.

"The continent is enormous," Owen continued, "and wholly indifferent to us. From my earliest boyhood, the vision of this vast and marvelous land has enchanted me. The way to make it fit for human habitation, I believed, was by science and law. But we have chosen another way, an older way." Through his mind marched the Roman legions, spears glinting. Perry's ships thundering on Lake Erie. Ely's brother peeling scalps. "We have claimed the land by force. The soles of our shoes are bloody."

The courtroom filled with murmurs. Owen raised his voice, as if calling into the wind: "Our children must live with the legacy of our violence, and so must their children, and so on down through the generations."

Fidgeting in his armchair, the judge declared impatiently, "I fail to catch the drift of your argument, Mr. Lightfoot."

"My point," said Owen, who had only the vaguest idea what point he was trying to make, but kept speaking to relieve the ache of disillusionment, "my point is that we must stop killing everyone and everything that stands in our way. We have the power to stop, right here and now with this man. In Columbus our State is building a penitentiary, which offers criminals the chance of reforming—a chance we deny any man forever by hanging him."

Man! the spectators echoed mockingly.

"It is true," Owen continued, shouting to make himself heard above the catcalls and whistles, "the defendant killed a man, a vicious man, but he did so in order to protect an innocent girl."

"An Indian witch!" someone cried.

The judge could not quiet the tumult for all his banging.

Owen clung to the railing of the jury box with both hands, leaning into the gale of hatred, shouting: "We were told yesterday by Mademoiselle Rozier—"

Cries of "Half-breed!" and "Witch!" burst from the crowd.

The giant swayed heavily on his bench, and the metal ringing of his chains hushed the audience. Ely grabbed him by the ear and tugged the bushy head around, signing for him to keep still. The onlookers held their breath. The deputies fingered their guns. But the big man did not rise.

"That's better," wheezed the judge, who took credit for stilling the crowd. "Sheriff," he said, pointing randomly into the audience, "remove those troublemakers."

Even after a few hecklers had been expelled from the room, Owen stood for a minute in flustered silence. Then he began, "We heard yesterday—" but the words dried on his tongue. He would bring no more shame on the law by pretending to reason with this rabble. These people had begun the trial as his neighbors, but they had become wrathful strangers. With a feeling of immense weariness, he concluded: "We are confronted today with the gravest task ever laid upon a community, that of deciding whether a man should live or die." *Man man man*, the audience took up the word again, louder this time, and twisted it scornfully. "A human being," Owen insisted hotly, "who has been played a nasty joke by nature—but nonetheless human. We must not take away his life merely because he is a mystery to us."

After the jury climbed into the attic of the courthouse, where they would discuss their verdict, Ely led the giant through the jammed aisle, down the stairs where children broke up a game of yarnball to tag along, and then clanking through the street to the jail. No sooner was the giant resting upon the cornshuck mattress, however, than a messenger arrived from the court to demand his return. So Ely led him back through the street, his iron steps encircled by children who peppered him with questions.

The big man took his seat. Ely held one of the great mitts between his own two hands. Judge Pond called for the verdict. The jury foreman rose through cottony silence to declare, "Your Honor, we find the accused guilty of murder in the first degree."

All eyes now fixed upon the giant, to detect in him some sign that their law had touched him. But he stared impassively into the crowd, his yellow eyes so blank they might have been chunks of sulfur. Defiance or anger would have served as well as fear to show the townspeople that he recognized at last the power of their collective will. But all that showed in his face was a monumental indifference, even when the judge, speaking in the ornate language of despised England, pronounced his sentence:

"It is considered by the court that the accused be

taken from hence to the jail of the County of Pilgrim, from whence he came, there to remain until the last Saturday of November next, being the twenty-ninth day of the month, on which day he be taken to the place of execution, between the hours of twelve o'clock at noon and two o'clock in the afternoon, and there to be hanged by the neck until he be dead."

18

DESPITE FROZEN ROADS AND THREATS OF SNOW, nearly a thousand people converged on Roma in the last week of November. Every cabin was crammed with guests, some from as far away as Kentucky. Visitors who could not find a floor to sleep on camped under wagons and in hasty lean-tos. The tavern ran out of food, and the shops emptied their shelves. There were dances and sermons at all hours, barkers selling potions, politicians shaking hands, fortune-tellers doing a brisk business. Anyone who had not heard about the execution might have thought Roma was hosting a fair.

In his cell, Ely ignored the festivities. By daylight and firelight men still kept watch in a ring around the jail, hugging rifles, imagining the boy and giant might try to escape. But Ely had passed beyond thoughts of escape or revenge, beyond despair, into an unforeseen tranquillity, as though, after canoeing through miles of rapids, he had drifted into calm water. Those who passed near the jail were surprised to hear him singing ballads about highwaymen, rustlers, pirates, assassins, every species of bad man. Those who peered in at the window were even more puzzled to discover the two of them, giant and boy, sleeping under the same heap of quilts, like big and little brothers.

Beside the scaffold in the village square, oblivious to the gawking crowds, Rain Hawk prepared the giant's grave. She laid out the boundaries east and west, obeying the path of the sun, and marked the corners with pegs. Before digging, she bathed herself in Bone Creek, breaking the ice, and rubbed a broth of cleansing herbs on her skin. On each cheek she painted a red circle, and around her neck she wore a necklace of white beans. For three days she dug the hole, letting no one else touch the shovel, buckskin wound about her hands to prevent blisters, and she lined the grave with slabs of elm bark. Once the wood had been gathered for the vigil fire, all that remained was the laying-out of the burial goods to aid the bearman on his journey, and then, in silence beside the grave, the fasting and waiting.

Owen nailed a piece of sacking over the hole in his door where the plate glass had been, to keep out the cold and to shield himself from the throngs in the street. He did not bother to replace the ATTORNEY sign, for he would attract no more clients in this town, nor did he want any. In the weeks between trial and execution he wound up his legal business, which included the sale of his office. For a time he thought of starting over in Columbus, down there at the hub of Ohio's wheel, but he could not fancy himself emulating men such as Fidelio Kingsbury and Moses Pond. Instead he arranged for two wagons to carry Mrs. Forbes and himself, his instruments, his books and furnishings back to Philadelphia. The West would have to rise or fall without him.

On the eve of the hanging Owen dressed in a plain black suit, the kind his father used to wear to Quaker meeting, and explained to Mrs. Forbes that he was going to say farewell to Ely. "Be careful of the mob, sweetheart," she cautioned him, "and don't be long." "I promise," he said, lifting the hair from her forehead to plant a kiss on the worry lines.

The square was full of tents and wagons and milling bodies. The focus of this multitude was the gallows, where Asher Gurley was testing the mechanism for the trapdoor. Owen found himself drawn into the crowd, watching the blacksmith tie a plowshare, an anvil, and a bucket of scrap iron to a thick rope that dangled from the crossbeam. When all was in readiness, he tramped down the stairs, springing the trap as he landed on the bottom step, whereupon the metal weights hurtled down, jouncing with a fearful clang as the rope jerked taut. The bystanders cheered.

"Reckon that'll do the trick, lawyer?" Gurley asked, wiping his hands on his apron while the iron jostled upon its rope.

"It is a most ingenious mechanism," Owen answered stiffly.

He stopped nearby to take his leave of Mademoiselle Rozier, who sat beside the open grave enveloped in blankets, only her calm face showing. Owen envied her serenity. He was convinced, by her songs and rituals, her knowledge of plants, her grace of movement, that she possessed an intuition of the world's order. As for himself, the longer he lived, the more chaotic the world appeared. He was about to speak, when a glance from her green eyes told him this was not a time for words. So he merely lifted a hand, as he had seen her do, as if feeling in the air for the invisible threads of starlight, and she returned the gesture, drawing a dusky hand from the blankets, and then he walked away.

Dodging campfires, stepping over the bedrolls of soldiers who had come to oversee the execution, Owen picked his way across the square to the jail, where an officer with one eye adroop from a saber wound let him pass without challenge. The guards had grown casual. Since charging out of court on the first day of the trial, the giant had remained quiet, only stirring when Ely told him to. Yet even in his quietness, the great man always seemed to Owen like a sleeping volcano. The twisted doorframe at the entrance of the cell was sufficient reminder of his strength.

Inside, Ely was sitting in a pool of lantern light, needle in hand, his lap covered by an enormous shirt of bleached linen on which he had been sewing for days. The giant lay in a pile of quilts, his face and one exposed hand glowing with a brilliance that startled Owen. The cell had an odor of soap and damp earth.

Looking up from his sewing, Ely said, "When do you leave?"

"At dawn."

Ely broke into one of his cockeyed smiles. "I'm glad to see I taught you that much, to get up early."

"You taught me a good deal more than that, my friend."

"It won't be the same Owen Lightfoot rolling back into Philadelphia as the one who left."

"Hardly." Overcome by a feeling of tenderness, Owen pressed his lips together against the itch of tears. He stood watching his comrade sew the white cloth. During the weeks of living in the giant's cell, Ely had become even more gaunt, whittled-down; the sockets of his eyes looked like charred knotholes. And yet to Owen he seemed newborn, as if all that the cruelty of men could hurt had been sloughed away, an old skin, and the surviving core of him were incorruptible. At length Owen trusted himself to say, "For one thing, there are about forty fewer pounds of flesh on me. And I have shed a comparable burden of illusions."

"You also got yourself a fine woman to wive," said Ely, "and that ain't a little gift."

"And you have Mademoiselle Rozier?"

"Or maybe she's got me. One way or the other, seems we been yoked together. Everything else has been tore away from us. I never thought I'd be figuring a girl in my future. But I believe I've grown into it."

"Where will the two of you go? To the Shawnee villages?"

"Naw," said Ely. "They kicked her out for having

white blood in her, back when this war started. And when she went home to fetch the funeral tobacco, with Tecumseh dead and all, they let her know she was worse medicine than ever."

"So she's been outcast by whites and Indians alike?"

"Just my kind of girl exactly," said Ely. "I'm an expert at living on the outside edge of things, scorned by everybody." Holding the cloth within a few inches of his face, he patiently sewed the linen shirt, as he had mended his moccasins before going up the cliff after the giant.

On the eve of the capture, just as now, on the eve of the execution, Owen had also given up, had reached a limit of courage or desire. "Are you sure you won't go back with me?"

Again came the unsettling smile. "Can't you just see her and me traipsing down the streets of Philadelphia? They'd hire us for a Wild West show, or stuff us and put us in that museum you was always going to."

"They might at that," Owen agreed. His heart was heavy, a weight greater than the iron dangling on the gallows, yet his partner's flare of humor gave him new courage. Sniffing the damp air of the cell, he said, "Do I smell soap?"

"I scrubbed him." Ely gestured with the needle toward a muddy patch on the earthen floor, where a hog-bristle brush leaned against a pail. Owen understood then why the giant's face and palm glowed so disturbingly. "As soon as I finish this sewing," Ely added, "I'm going to comb the snarls out of that mane and trim his beard and dress him in new clothes. He's going to be a sight to see tomorrow, let me tell you."

Reaching out with a shoe, Owen prodded the heap of rawhide garments near the bucket, the leather stained and scratched, reeking still with the giant's odor. "You mean to shame them?"

"I mean for them to see what sort of man they're killing, how fine he is, how far beyond them."

"Once you have him ready, can't you leave—" Owen's voice was drowned by an iron clanging as the blacksmith tested his trapdoor again, the anvil and plowshare and bucket clapping together like tuneless bells. Owen tried again: "Couldn't you turn him over to the sheriff in the morning, and leave before noon?"

"You know I can't do that." Ely jabbed his needle through the pale cloth. "I don't want him to die like a bull at a butcher's. I got to see him decently hanged and them all shamed doing it, and then I got to help Rain Hawk bury him."

"Will he know the difference?" said Owen.

"It don't matter what he knows." Ely stood up, holding the linen shirt by the shoulders so that it hung smooth, broad as a sheet. "It matters what I know. And I know how he got found out in his killing, how he was tracked down and caught in the cave and led back here. I know what's waiting for him tomorrow, and I'm going to stick around long enough to see him through it."

"But why torture yourself needlessly?"

"It ain't needless!" Ely cried vehemently. Then in a tone of consolation he added, "Mr. Lightfoot, you're a good man, so good you been spat on for living up to your conscience. You've been a daily surprise to me, and stretched my mind by a couple of acres. When we set out I didn't think you were much at all; but I learned different. I learned to respect what you've got in your head and in your heart. But that don't alter the fact that you and me are put together different, bred for different soils. I wish it wasn't so. But it is. You just got to accept it."

Owen did accept it, and kept his peace.

At a nod from Ely, the giant rose from his mound of quilts, hunching over to avoid the beams. He was naked to the waist, wearing only the moccasins and woollen breeches Ely had made for him. The skin of his chest gleamed through the mat of iron-dark hair, almost as if the flesh were illuminated from within. His nakedness made him seem more human, more vulnerable. Veins showed in his throat, breath swelled his belly, the muscles joined together at his shoulders like any man's, only on a grander scale. Stooping there, he seemed too large for the shirt Ely was measuring against him. When at last it was tugged on over his head, he filled it to bursting. Owen could even make out, beneath the gauzy cloth, the sluggish heartbeat.

Ely gave the giant one of his lopsided grins, half smile and half grimace. "That will dazzle them, big fellow. Now for that mane of yours." The giant squatted down and stared at the lantern while Ely worked the knots from his hair with the bristle brush. When the black mane lay smooth about the moon face, Ely dipped his finger in a stone pestle and smeared a daub of red paint on the bearman's forehead, and then on his own.

Watching them—the spindly, fierce boy circling about the placid giant—Owen remembered the two of them climbing down from the cave, identical necklaces rattling on their chests and red smears on their foreheads, such odd brothers, and he felt once more like an intruder. It was time to go. How to postpone saying good-bye? "It's miserably cold," he said.

"It's what my pappy called hog-killing weather," Ely said. "Anything you slaughter now will keep till spring."

Owen blinked at his partner. The trail they had shared ached inside him. "Here," he said, handing Ely a clasp-topped purse. "I wanted to give you something."

A flicker of the old fury showed in Ely's face. "I can get by without any gift of money."

"It isn't money," said Owen.

Ely accepted the purse and opened it. Inside were seeds, glistening brown drops like bits of dark fire. "Is it apples?"

"It's an orchard's worth of winesaps, the finest apples I ever tasted in Ohio. You and Mademoiselle Rozier can plant them when you get established somewhere. I wanted you to take something fruitful away from this place, something better . . ." Owen stammered into silence.

Ely tried to speak, but had to give it up for a few seconds. Meanwhile, Owen looked out through the ruined window, blinking against the sting in his eyes.

Campfires splashed yellow onto the darkness. When Ely's voice emerged, it was as soft as rain: "We'll plant them one of these days, Mr. Lightfoot. I promise you. We'll head west until we find a place beyond the borders of war and slavery and hate, and we'll settle there, build us a cabin, and raise the sweetest apples in all the wilderness."

Owen forced a smile. "If you ride west far enough and I ride east, maybe we'll meet?"

"You never know. Just keep following your compass."

"Peace to you." Owen raised his hand and swept the air, to include the giant in his farewell.

"Peace, brother." Ely dipped his finger again in the stone pestle, and brought it out slick with paint, and daubed a red spot on Owen's forehead.

The partners touched hands, and Ely wrapped Owen in a rough and wordless and grieving hug, and then they were apart, apart most likely forever, and Ely was snipping at the giant's wiry beard with a pair of shears, and Owen was hurrying away from the jail, the paint on his forehead burning like a brand.

19

O N THE DAY OF THE EXECUTION, ROMA FROZE. ICE
crept over the mouths of wells, over rain barrels
and water troughs. Noontime brought sun but no
warmth. Waiting for the prisoner to emerge from jail,
people fed their fires and stood upon heated bricks,
fingers stiff inside rag mittens, their mouths haloed by
a fog of breath. Spectators eager for a view of the
gallows defied the bitter wind to balance on the roof-
tops of cabins and in the limbs of trees. Wrapped in
blankets, others watched from horseback and wagon
beds and upended barrels. The arrival of winter had
not chilled their spirits. Squealing children were passed
from hand to hand over the heads of the crowd, an
organ-grinder played, war veterans shouted greetings
to old comrades. But as the hour ticked past noon the
door of the jail opened, and a hush spread through
the crowd, the way ice knits crystal webs through
water.

The fellow who emerged from the jail was a dis-
appointment. He was a boy, really, not so very tall,

and scrawny as a fence post. His ragged deerhide clothes hung on him like the skin on a starving wolf. His face, encircled by flame-red hair, was not the least bit mean or murderous; it looked as though it had been scrubbed clean of all feeling. What sort of prodigy was this supposed to be? The stories whispering through the backwoods had led them to expect a gigantic monster with fangs and webbed fingers. Who was this scraggly boy? The answer quickly spread through the crowd: Ely Jackson, that was who, a moody, orphaned wanderer, the giant's only friend.

For all their imagining ahead of time, the onlookers were not prepared for the next creature who squeezed through the doorway of the jail. None of the rumors had stretched their minds wide enough to hold this wonder. The noon sun dazzled from the expanse of bleached linen across his chest. A necklace of teeth blazed about his throat. His flesh seemed radiant. Men elbowed one another aside to get a better view. Women who had tarried on the edges of the crowd to avoid betraying any interest in the hanging now pushed shamelessly through the ranks of men in order to catch a nearer glimpse of this dazzling man. Iron-dark hair glistened in waves to his shoulders and the pitch-black beard clustered in tight curls along his jaw. None of the watchers had ever seen such eyes before, eyes like fire glimpsed away off through the woods. Even though his arms were bound with chains, he did not seem like a captive, but like an ambassador visiting from a more splendid country.

The giant gazed down upon the soldiers, the tethered horses, and the hundreds of awestruck faces as he followed Ely toward the gallows. Behind them came a half-breed squaw, sweeping their footsteps from the dust with a broom of twigs. This was Rain Hawk, the local people whispered, refusing to use her white name since she had spoken in court. The men caught their breaths, looking at her, and the women puzzled over God's reason for pouring so much beauty into such a low-born vessel. Behind her marched a dozen militiamen, rifles on their shoulders. They had to stretch their paces to keep up with the giant, for he marched to the gallows without any hesitation.

Ely stopped near the base of the stairs, but at a sign from him the giant climbed straight up onto the scaffold, ignoring the dignitaries in their uniforms, the minister in a black gown, and the colonel with badges on his chest. The hangman, wearing a gunnysack for a hood, waited on the scaffold beside the trapdoor, holding the noose, and the militiamen took up positions along the four sides. Aloft upon the scaffold, the prisoner seemed even more colossal. Many of those watching, awed by his size and dignity and his candle-flame eyes, found it hard to believe that he would actually be killed. He was too magnificent for death. Something more could be made of him, surely.

The Methodist minister ascended the stairs and recited his prayers; then, receiving no acknowledgment from the prisoner, he climbed back down again. That left the militia colonel and the hooded hangman, looking puny by comparison, alone upon the scaffold with the giant.

Now he should make his speech, those experienced at hangings were saying; now he should confess his crimes or proclaim his innocence. Yet he stood there mute. To the road-weary people who were seeing him for the first time, he did not seem incapable of speech. He merely seemed unwilling to humble himself by talking. And if he spoke at all, his language would be foreign, a strange dialect never before heard in this territory.

Beholding him, men felt shabby in their weathered clothes, and vowed to have new ones made when they returned home; they resolved to cut larger windows into their cabins, chop bigger clearings into the woods, drain swamps, and build solid barns, all of this to ease the ache which the splendid prisoner had roused in their hearts. The women, many of them cloaked in veils, suddenly felt Roma huddling around them in all its dinginess and poverty, and they vowed to paint doors and plant flowering trees and make their children stand up tall when they returned home.

Above the giant's head the noose spun idly, as if stirred by the breath from all these watching faces. He cast his tranquil gaze over them like a benediction, over the heads of the waiting soldiers, over the cabins and carts and horses in harness, over the stark, leafless branches of the encircling forest, and then he fixed his stare on Ely. For a few hurtful seconds, Ely returned the stare, thinking, Forgive us. The giant's breath flowered about his face, yet he did not seem cold, waiting there for death; he seemed to glow with an inner flame, calm, untouchable. Only when the hangman climbed onto a stool and tried to slip the noose over his iron-dark head did he show a flicker of bewilderment.

At that moment Ely's heart cracked open with grief and he let out a bellow of pain. The great dazzling man bellowed in reply. With a single contemptuous shrug he burst the chains holding his wrists, swatted the hangman and colonel aside, and then he charged across the platform toward Ely, arms flung wide in a blaze of white. Seeing him come, the people behind Ely cleared an avenue. In an instant the crowd was clapping and whistling. "Make way! Make way!" they cried, imagining he might seize Ely under one arm and Rain Hawk under the other and stride right away from his death, away to his own far country.

But the colonel scrambled to his feet and shouted, "Fire!" and the soldiers obeyed. The air shook. Smoke plumed from a dozen rifles. The giant balanced on the edge of the scaffold, red splotches riddling his white shirt, and then he thundered to earth like a felled tree. Ely threw himself on top of him, sobbing, and the spice girl bent over the two of them. Everyone else drew back, to give the giant air, to allow him space to rise. But the huge body lay motionless, the necklace glittering icily over one shoulder, the white shirt, which had dazzled moments before in the sunlight, now sobering with blood, the tree-limb arms flung to either side with hanks of chain still attached, the face now as calm, as alien, as it had been before death, the yellow eyes open to the sky.

For a long time the only sound came from Ely, who wailed and thrashed like an animal in a trap.

Rain Hawk tore the giant's shirt into rags and used them to cleanse the blood from his chest. The onlookers were slow in believing that so much creature could die so quickly, but the fact gradually soaked in, and everyone, even the soldiers, withdrew in shocked silence. Citizens of Roma vanished into cabins and sheds. People who had journeyed there to see the monster die now fled from town with no more noise than the creaking of wagons, the slap of leather, the thud of hoof on stone.

20

THE WAYS OF THE SPIRIT WORLD, KNOWN TO RAIN Hawk from her mother, guided their last dealings with the giant. We must wash the blood from his chest, she told Ely. Prop him up so that I can scrub him. Cut the buttons from his breeches. Wipe the dust from his moccasins. Now hold his face while I paint the spots of fire on his cheeks, the streaks of lightning at the corners of his eyes. You must draw the shape of a hand on his chest, so the powers will know we have sent him. Here, dip your finger in this clay and paint the gray hand on his chest. Now we must dress him in his new buckskin shirt, make him ready for his long journey.

Ely did as she told him, touching the scorned body, feeling numb and dazed. He even fetched a key from the sheriff, in order to unlock the manacles from the giant's wrists. There must be no metal in the grave, Rain Hawk said. Obeying her, Ely moved like a sleepwalker. The air was bitterly cold, yet the chill he felt was deeper than weather.

We must comb his hair, she said. There, like so, make it lie smooth about his face. Now it is time to light the fire beside the grave. You do it, for it must not go out once it sparks, and your hands are sure on the flint.

Cupping the shredded grapevine bark in his palm, Ely struck steel against flint as he had done hundreds of times, only now he took the greatest care that the tinder should catch on the first spark and stay lit, and he thrust the handful of fire beneath the kindling she had prepared, and he puffed gently, and it blazed up.

Once the flame was steady, Rain Hawk said, "You must speak to him before we lay him in the ground."

"Can't you do it?" he begged.

"It must be a man who speaks."

"But I don't have any notion what to say."

"I will tell you, and then you must tell him."

Frozen, mumbling as though his jaw were locked with cold, Ely stood over the great body and repeated her words: "Go on your way, Bear Walks, and do not come back to trouble us. We will keep watch over you, and feed you, and light your way to the other world. Go home to Our Grandmother, big one. Do not be angry with us. Go in peace."

Hard as they pulled, they could not drag the body to the grave. Ely had to untie the rope from the gallows, saddle his mare, loop one end of the rope about the giant's feet and the other about the saddle horn, and tug at the reins while Rain Hawk guided the body over the ground. When at last the giant rolled into the bark-lined grave, he landed faceup, his feet toward the east, head to the west. Rain Hawk reached down and crossed the arms on his chest, grunting from the weight. Then she laid the few gifts beside him—the clay pot filled with corn, the basket of wheat, foxtail, eagle feather, stick of ironwood.

From beneath her apron she drew out a small doe-skin pouch and held it open before Ely. "Take a pinch of the tobacco," she said, "and walk around the grave, bending low, like so, and sprinkle it on the body."

They circled the grave three times, Ely going before, Rain Hawk behind, scattering tobacco until the giant was dusted with the brown shreds. Toward evening, as snow flurried down through the darkening air, the body was dusted white. It seemed cruel to leave him uncovered, Ely thought, but Rain Hawk insisted he must be left so until the following noon. They washed their faces and hands in a broth of herbs, ate the food she had cooked during her week of fasting, and kept their vigil the first night, huddled over the funeral fire. When Ely could not stop shivering, she wrapped her blanket around both of them and held him close, her fingers warm inside his shirt.

From the moment of the shooting, the townspeople had kept their distance, lurking in cabins, hastening by on the wooden sidewalks, avoiding the square. Every now and again, as he watched over the body, Ely would look up to see them stealing past or peering from windows. It surprised him that he felt no hatred toward them, no anger, as though he had swum a river that washed away all feeling. He did not even shout at them when they asked how long this business would take. "Three days," was all he answered. "And then you'll be shut of us."

On the morning of the second day, two men wearing stovepipe hats, black suits, and waxed moustaches walked up to the grave. They identified themselves as doctors from Hudson Academy, and offered ten dollars for the giant's body.

Ely felt a tingle of rage along his nerves, the first cracks in his inward ice. "What you want him for?"

"To discover the secret of his remarkable size," one of the doctors replied.

"Discover how? You mean cut him up?"

The doctors raised their offer to fifteen dollars.

"Cut him *up?*" Ely roared. "It ain't enough that he's dead, you got to hack him to bits? I'll show you cutting! Where's my knife?"

In a low, earnest voice, Rain Hawk said to the doctors, "You should go," and they withdrew hastily.

Not long after, while Ely's temper was cooling, a Dutch Reformed missionary rode up on a mule to offer a new provocation. He had heard about the giant in Pittsburgh, he explained, and, figuring from what people said about the giant's odd speech that the unfortunate man was Dutch, he had come to take the body home for Christian burial. The missionary did not stay quite as long as the doctors. Ely roasted his ears and threatened his life, and meant every word of it, he was so furious. Mule and rider cantered away.

The last frozen backwaters inside Ely thawed on that second day, when a wagon rolled in from Cleveland carrying two men who wanted to buy the corpse for a traveling carnival. The back of the wagon was loaded down with a green slab of Lake Erie ice and buried in sawdust. They would just lay the giant on the ice and drive him through the countryside from village to village. A valuable exhibit, they said, a wonder of nature. They had not quite finished their explanation when Ely flung a fistful of stones at their heads, and they, too, beat a hasty retreat.

After the grinding of their wheels had died away, he said to Rain Hawk, "We got to bury him, before I hurt somebody."

"Now is the time," she agreed.

They covered the body with elm bark, starting with the feet. Ely hesitated before placing the last slab of bark, gazing at the blank face, the painted cheeks and eyes, beard combed smooth, flecks of snow and tobacco on the frozen skin. This last glimpse stirred up in him a whirlwind of memories—the stump out front of Rain Hawk's hut, the gigantic bootprints, the hunt with Owen, the cave, the trial, the final shooting. Unable to bear it, Ely gently rested the bark on the enormous, outlandish, extinguished face, and then he and Rain Hawk took turns shoveling. When the grave was heaped high, she swept the surrounding earth, removing their footprints and all scars of the spade.

Ely felt inwardly each sweep of her broom, as if she were smoothing his pain. The funeral gestures were a comfort to him, easing him past the giant's death, as they eased the giant himself on his journey. Yet this bare mound seemed too paltry a sign of the bearman's passing. Ely wanted to erect a wooden cross, or even to lay a ring of stones around the grave; but she said no. There must be no mark aside from the heaped soil.

Shivering, splashing their faces with tea when they felt sleepy, they kept their vigil through a second night and a third day. Ely fed sticks to the fire. Rain Hawk chanted prayers.

The people of Roma resumed their lives, but gave the pair a wide berth, as though the grave and the two watchers were an island in a river, lifted above the town's current. Men took down the scaffold, hauling the planks away.

On the third night, Rain Hawk served the giant his last meal, placing cornbread and beans and roasted rabbit on the mound of dirt. All through the dark hours she told the tales of her people, about the beginning and end of things, about Our Grandmother the creator and her Grandson, about Thunderbird and Cyclone Person, Corn Woman, the Giant Horned Snakes, about the Four Winds, the Moon, the Earth, and all the mysteries of the universe. She only quit speaking at dawn, the moment for the spirit of Bear Walks to depart, when nothing earthly could touch him.

"Now you must speak to him again," she told Ely.

This time as he spoke, Ely felt every turn of the words, as if they were birds flying through the caves of his heart, and he felt ready to set the spirit of the bearman free: "Go home, brother. Go to Our Grandmother. Do not look back, do not turn around to trouble us. Go in peace, big one."

All that remained was for Ely and Rain Hawk to

wash their hair in water heated over the funeral fire, and then to comb it down, down, like the fall of rain, and then to roll everything they owned into saddle blankets and mount their horses and ride away toward the unpeopled lands, never looking back, not wanting to anger the dead, and on their journey to begin learning one another's songs.

Afterword

Of all my books, this wild, shaggy novel had the longest gestation. It was conceived in July 1974, when I happened upon a description of an early murder case from the county in northeastern Ohio where I had grown up, and it was published, after many rejections and revisions, in September 1986. During the dozen years between conception and birth, the original story, bizarre enough to begin with, took on the qualities of myth.

The seed of the story lay in the pages of a fat volume bound in cloth the color of plums and entitled *History of Portage County, Ohio*, which I came across while browsing the stacks of the Indiana University library. The title caught my eye, for I had lived in Portage County from age five through seventeen, and I could not imagine that enough had ever happened in this out-of-the-way place to fill such a thick tome. Taking the book from the shelf, I opened at random to Chapter XI, which began this way: "All organized communities, it matters not what may be their geographical location or their general moral and religious status, have criminal records, some of which are replete with deeds of violence and bloodshed, while others are not so bad." Intrigued by the promise of bloody deeds and amused by the "not so bad" disclaimer, I sat down on the cool tile floor of the library and kept reading.

Within a few paragraphs, I learned about the murder

in 1814 of a peddler named Epaphras Mathews by Henry Aunghst,

> a man of powerful muscular organization and great strength. He was a foundry-man, or iron-worker, by trade, but naturally sluggish in his motions and movements. It was told of him that when at work in Pittsburgh he would pick up a trip-hammer, weighing 500 pounds, and lift it into an old-fashioned Pennsylvania wagon.

This iron man rose to 6'7", impressive enough in our day but a towering figure at a time when a full-grown man might have stood 5'3" or 5'5". The trial revealed that Aunghst had accompanied the peddler from Pittsburgh into Ohio, selling goods to homesteaders and turning over the money to Mathews. When they arrived at a fork in the road east of Ravenna—a place known as Cotton Corners when I was growing up, home to a drive-in where I drank my first cup of coffee—Aunghst evidently decided the loot should be his, for he stove in the peddler's head with an ironwood stake, relieved the body of $270 in coin, which he tied up in a handkerchief, then set off for Pittsburgh. Two men from Ravenna, Lewis Ely and Robert Eaton, tracked him down and hauled him back for trial, receiving "$222.87 for their services and damages inflicted upon their horses."

While awaiting trial, Aunghst broke out of the log jail one day when the jailer's wife came in to fetch a spinning wheel. She spread the alarm, and he was soon recaptured, laughing and puffing. During the trial itself, Aunghst signaled that he could neither speak nor understand English, even though, according to witnesses, he conversed "glibly enough with the school children who would stand upon a barrel and talk through the iron grating covering the window of his cell." He was duly convicted and sentenced to hang in the main street of Ravenna.

The militia was called out to stand guard on the day of his execution. The noose did not break his neck, so the 1,800 people who showed up for the spectacle got to watch him strangle. The body was buried near the foot of the scaffold, right there in the street where I used to visit the library and the five-and-dime as a boy. That night the corpse was dug up and spirited away—"for anatomical purposes," people suspected—and the townsfolk set out to bring it back. After a second burial, a "party of German residents," claiming Aunghst as one of their own, stole the body with plans for sinking it in a nearby pond, to "keep it from the doctors." Once more the body was recovered, and a sheriff's posse guarded it through the night. The following day it was "re-interred in the original grave, the coffin being filled with lime, and the largest log possible placed upon it." In spite of these precautions, rumors continued to circulate that the doctors had got their bloody hands on the body after all.

The plum-colored book in which I found this curious history must have survived a fire sometime between its publication in Chicago in 1885 and that summer of 1974, for the pages smelled of smoke. By the time I read of the third burial, the smell had set me thinking of campfires, and I was imagining two mismatched deputies trailing a huge man through the backwoods. The fugitive loomed so large in my imagination that he began to resemble Bigfoot, the hairy, shambling, elusive creature known to native people around the world as Yeti, Omee, Sasquatch. As the novel took form, first in my head, then in my journal, then on sheets of paper dimpled by the worn keys of my typewriter, the peddler grew smaller and crueler, the iron man grew larger and stranger, and the tales stirred up by their passage through the Ohio frontier became ever more fabulous.

On the frontier, that ragged margin where settlers of European descent met the wilderness, anything seemed possible. There were stories about seven-foot-long human skeletons dug up in the burial mounds of the Ohio Valley. There were stories about girls kidnapped from cabins and married off to bears. There were stories about blue-eyed, blond-haired Indians who spoke Welsh. There were stories about the lost tribes of Israel, survivors from Atlantis, strayed Vikings, and giants, all wandering out there in the wilds. When President Jefferson sent Lewis and Clark to find a route to the Pacific in 1803, he instructed them to watch for woolly mammoths, whose bones had been found in the salt licks of Kentucky. A decade later, just when the events recounted in *Bad Man Ballad* were unfolding, John James Audubon thought he heard the bellowing of these great beasts from canebrakes on the lower stretches of the Ohio River. Who could say what creatures lurked in the deep woods, the rolling prairies, the distant mountains?

The American wilderness had fascinated me since childhood, especially the hardwood forests of the heartland, bounded to the east by the Appalachian Mountains, to the north by the Great Lakes, and to the west by the Great Plains. As a boy I read everything I could find about the Indians of that vast inland region, including the mysterious people who had raised earthworks in the shape of serpents and birds. I read about the explorers who filled in blank spaces on the maps, the naturalists who described species new to science, the hunters and trappers, the woodsmen, the pioneers. I was dazzled by the daring, the strength and ingenuity, and the sheer backbreaking labor that had turned the wild woods into the tamed world of towns and farms and roads. But I also ached over the loss of wildness, the felling of ancient trees, the murder and expulsion of Indians, the slaughter of wolves and lions and bears.

Even as a boy, I sensed that the defining fact of our nation's history was the war against wilderness—against native people, against predators and varmints, against shadowy forests and unbroken grasslands, against free-flowing rivers and overflowing swamps, against heat and cold and bugs and disease, against any creature or scruple or force that would thwart our ambition or defy our control. And what was our ambition? To create for ourselves and our children a land of milk and honey, a new Eden, prosperous and comfortable and safe. In pursuit of that goal, our ancestors enslaved millions of Africans, waged war at home and abroad, imprisoned dissidents, all the while proclaiming that the Creation exists purely to serve us, to fill our bellies with food, our eyes with scenery, our pockets with money.

From the moment I stumbled upon the account of that bizarre murder case, I saw the iron man as a visitor from the wilderness. *Wilderness*, in fact, was my working title for the novel I began writing in the fall of 1974. That September, my wife and I moved, along with our twenty-month-old daughter, Eva, to New Hampshire, where I began a year's residency as the Bennett Writing Fellow at

Phillips Exeter Academy. At the time, I had published ten or fifteen stories in magazines, but no books of fiction, so the Academy showed remarkable faith in my promise by granting me a year's freedom to write. They offered a stipend, invited us to meals in the dining hall, and provided lodging for my family at the edge of campus in a fine old house furnished with antiques. Ivy curled at the windows. Mice scratched in the walls. The floorboards creaked at every footfall. Now and again bats emerged from the fireplace and flitted through the room I used as a study. It was the ideal setting to dream up a story about an almost legendary past.

All the Academy asked in return was that I share my work with students. So I visited classes once or twice a week to read aloud chapters of the novel as I completed them. When I visited one class for the first time, a boy asked me, "Mr. Sanders, are you going to read us literature, or something you wrote yourself?" "Something I wrote myself," I admitted. Indeed, I had never read my own work in public before, and I can still hear those audiences laughing or taking in a nervous breath as they followed the story, I can still see the dreamy, faraway look in their eyes as they listened. After hearing the early installments, students would halt me on walkways under the huge elms to ask what happened next, and I would tell them honestly that I didn't know, that I would only find out by writing my way to the end.

I reached the end of a first draft in December, by which time the story had diverged in significant ways from the bare facts of the murder case. I had named the town Roma instead of Ravenna, and the county Pilgrim instead of Portage, to allow for the borrowing of features from other settlements. I had shifted the date of the murder a year earlier, to August of 1813, in order to set the novel firmly in the midst of the war against the English and their Indian allies. I added a foot or so to the iron man's already daunting height, took away his capacity for speech, replaced his German name with the name of Bear Walks borrowed from the Chippewa, and instead of sending him east to Pittsburgh I sent him west, into wilder country.

The deputies who pursued the giant had to be invented almost entirely from scratch, since they appeared for only a couple of sentences in the original account. The differences between Owen Lightfoot and Ely Jackson—the one bookish, the other illiterate; the one living through his head, the other through his body; the one a city man, the other a backwoodsman—made for comedy as well as strife. The humor is there as much for my sake as for the reader's, because it helped me face the darkness at the heart of the story.

The novel is tragic, not merely because the giant dies, but because his death is part of our nation's long assault on wildness—on native people, animals, our own sexual bodies, on soil and water and sky. I mean for Bear Walks to be a character rather than a symbol, however enigmatic, but he is also powerful, wayward, mute, by turns benign and threatening, like the weather or the woods. The settlers wind up slaughtering him to relieve their fear, just as they cut down the trees and drive off the Indians and kill off troublesome beasts. Only after the giant has been shot do people realize what a grand, if scary, creature he was. Likewise, only after the woods have been leveled and the swamps drained and the predators extinguished do we begin to realize what has been lost.

While the townspeople of Roma were on edge because of the war with England, the war that troubled me as I composed the novel was the one recently concluded in Vietnam, the defining political drama of my coming-of-age. I kept asking myself why we had gone to war, sent hundreds of thousands of soldiers, spent billions upon billions of dollars, to impose our will on a poor, weak peasant people half the world away. What could explain this desire to dominate, this penchant for violence, this willingness to spend our blood and money and tears?

My reading of history, American and otherwise, revealed that people will do almost anything when they are afraid. The Salem witch trials, the whipping of rebellious slaves, the massacre of buffalo to starve Plains Indians into obedience, lynchings by the Ku Klux Klan, the shooting of union strikers by company thugs, the imprisonment of socialists during World War I, the internment of Japanese Americans during World War II, the McCarthyite persecution of dissidents during the 1950s, right up to the erosion of civil liberties and the waging of wars by our government today in the name of fighting terrorism—all of these episodes show how ready we have been to compromise our ideals, to set aside our moral standards, in the face of dread.

For all the darkness in the novel, my life was joyful in the spring of 1975 as I wrote the second draft. That January Eva turned two, and she was learning words so fast she seemed to be possessed by language. My wife, Ruth, looked after her in the mornings while I made sentences, then I took Eva for walks in the afternoons. Our favorite destination was a bridge overlooking a waterfall in the Squamscott River, site of the mill that led to the founding of Exeter. Eva and I would often stay there for an hour at a time, listening to the falls, while she told me fanciful stories, made up songs, or danced. I suspect it was these outings with my darling daughter, more than any artistic purpose, that inspired me to add the spice girl in the second draft of the novel. She acquired Eva's whimsical voice, her penchant for singing and storytelling, her bountiful, beautiful spirit.

Once admitted to the story, the spice girl took on a life of her own. With her double name, she straddled the border between whites and Indians, an outcast from both sides. As Mademoiselle Rozier, she carried a legacy from the French trappers and traders, the *coureurs du bois*—the runners of the woods—who had made themselves at home in the neighborhood of the Great Lakes long before the coming of the English. As Rain Hawk, she brought into the novel something of the vision and practice of the Shawnee, including the burial rites that she and Ely Jackson perform at the end of the novel.

Eva also accounted indirectly for the novel's eventual title. Each night while Ruth gave her a bath, I sat on the edge of the tub, playing my guitar and crooning selections from an anthology of American folksongs. One night I read in the editor's note that the songs celebrating colorful outlaws such as Jesse James or Billy the Kid or Stagolee were called "bad man ballads," and I realized I had found the true title for the novel I had been calling *Wilderness*.

I hoped that the "Ballad" in my new title would give me license to let my story roam beyond the bounds of strict realism, as folksongs do. The skirmishes and the movements of militias are faithful to the historical record, and so is the atmosphere of dread that envelops the settlers, but nobody living where my fictional Roma is located could have heard the thundering of guns from Perry's battle on Lake Erie. You'll find on a map of frontier Ohio nearly all of the places the deputies pass through, but don't go looking for Door-in-Rock, the cave where they catch up with the giant. The artifacts that Bear Walks shows to Ely are the sorts of things found in burial mounds along the Ohio River, and there are plenty of caverns in the limestone of southern Indiana, but the catacomb in my novel is imaginary. Some of the feats attributed to the giant by people who met him along his path might easily have occurred, while others belong to legend. With luck, this great and mysterious man, who occupied my imagination for so many years, will live on after me in that borderland where history gives way to myth.

Scott Russell Sanders

is the author of eighteen books, including
Staying Put, Hunting for Hope, and
The Force of Spirit. For his work in nonfiction,
he has won the Lannan Literary Award and
the John Burroughs Essay Award.
In all of his books he is concerned with our place
in nature, the pursuit of social justice, the character
of community, and the search for a spiritual path.
He is Distinguished Professor of English
at Indiana University. He and his wife, Ruth,
a biochemist, have reared two children in
their hometown of Bloomington, in the
hardwood hill country of the White River Valley.